PENGUIN CRIME FICTION
Editor: Julian Symons

THE SECOND CURTAIN

Roy Broadbent Fuller was born in Failsworth in 1912. A famous poet and author, he has had a distinguished career both as a solicitor for the Woolwich Equitable Building Society of which he is now a director and as Professor of Poetry at the University of Oxford (1968–73). He is now Vice-President of the Building Societies Association and has edited *The Building Societies Acts*. From 1941 to 1946 he served in the Royal Navy, becoming a lieutenant in 1944.

Among his many publications are *Savage Gold* (Puffin 1946), *With My Little Eye* (Peacock 1948), *Fantasy and Fugue* (1954), *Image of a Society* (1956) and *The Father's Comedy* (1961), all of which have been published in Penguins. Among his more recent publications are *Collected Poems* (1962), *New Poems* (1968) which won the Duff Cooper Memorial Prize in the same year, *Off Course* (1969), *The Carnal Island* (1970), *Owls and Artificers: Oxford Lectures in Poetry* (1971), *Seen Grandpa Lately?* (1972), *Tiny Tears* (1973) and *Professor and Gods: Last Oxford Lectures on Poetry* (1973).

Roy Fuller is Director of the Poetry Book Society and a Governor of the B.B.C. He is also a Fellow of the Royal Society of Literature and was awarded the C.B.E. and the Queen's Gold Medal for Poetry in 1970. He is married and has one son.

GW00992256

THE SECOND CURTAIN

ROY FULLER

Penguin Books

Penguin Books Ltd, Harmondsworth, Middlesex, England
Penguin Books Inc., 7110 Ambassador Road, Baltimore, Maryland 21207, U.S.A.
Penguin Books Australia Ltd, Ringwood, Victoria, Australia
Penguin Books Canada Ltd, 41 Steelcase Road West, Markham, Ontario, Canada
Penguin Books (N.Z.) Ltd, 182–190 Wairau Road, Auckland 10, New Zealand

—

First published by Verschoyle 1953
Published in Penguin Books 1962
Reprinted 1976

—

Made and printed in Great Britain
by Hazell Watson & Viney Ltd,
Aylesbury, Bucks
Set in Monotype Van Dijck

TO JOHN LEHMANN

Between bright eyes the bulbous nose:
Between the poetry the prose.
Enemies and lovers value eyes:
Nose is for all to recognize.

Chapter One

FOX was rather like a fox. Wings of red hair were brushed behind pointed ears: under the flat, bald skull the face was wide but sharp and startlingly young, with a large mouth that in grinning one half expected a pink tongue to loll out of. Garner, the other man at the table, was also in his early forties. He was thick-set and graceless. He directed his gaze past Fox's head, through the curtains and into Percy Street, until Fox had finished talking in Italian to the waiter and his embarrassment and sense of inferiority were a little relieved. He wondered why he should feel embarrassed when it was Fox who was the b.f.

The waiter went away. Fox turned intimately to Garner. 'We see nothing of you these days, George.'

Garner grunted.

'What are you doing now, George?'

Garner put a large piece of bread in his mouth and said, indistinctly: 'Reading for Cuffs again.' He had once known Fox quite well but he had never been on easy terms with him. Not that he was on easy terms with anyone, except those slight acquaintances like his tobacconist who had never tried to penetrate the formidable exterior and found the bog of shyness inside.

'No new novel?' Fox asked.

'No new novel.'

'Well, in a quite immorally selfish way, I'm glad.'

At this implication of the value of his work Garner crossed his legs uneasily under the table, rattling the cutlery. Fox speared a rectangle of ravioli, gazed at it intently, and then popped it into his fox's mouth.

'Very glad,' he said. 'As I hinted on the telephone, I've rather an important proposal to make to you, George, and I hoped you would be free from other commitments.'

Garner managed to be astringent – the astringency that always surprised and pleased him. 'You sound very portentous, Roderick.' Only in such a tone could he bring himself to utter the rather ridiculous syllables of Fox's Christian name. And as they came out, Fox's character rose in its coy nudity before him. Fox the Anthologist, the author of that one interminable poem in *vers libre*, ubiquitous President of the Guild of Letters. How stupid it was to envy him his manners, his education, money, confidence, and ability to speak Italian. Garner reminded himself of his own powers, and as their hands met for an instant reaching for the French mustard he compared Fox's white claw to its disadvantage with his own brown fist – the hand he thought of, in his frequently unguarded moments, as that of a craftsman.

The waiter came with a bottle of Algerian wine and obsequiously showed Fox the label. Fox carried off the absurdity with graceful aplomb, as though the wine had been a Château Mouton Rothschild, and Garner's little bubble of exaltation burst.

'I must tell you first of all,' said Fox, tasting the purplish meniscus the waiter had dropped into his glass, and nodding sagely, 'that there exists – outside all probability – a certain cultured captain of industry. He is rich and rather mad. And he is prepared to lose some money – quite a lot of money – on the arts. He doesn't want his name to be known at this stage. So I shall call him P.'

Fox paused for his effect and said: 'P thinks of financing a literary magazine.'

Garner cut a potato in half.

'It's quite astonishing,' Fox went on. 'P simply came to the G of L and named the sum he was thinking of putting down annually for five years. The sort of benefactor we all dreamed about in our twenties.'

The suspense was causing Garner discomfort. 'Where do I come in?' he said, without looking up.

'Editor, George,' said Fox, leaning far over his braised beef.

'Very kind,' muttered Garner.

'Nonsense, George. You're the obvious man – the only man. I just wish it had happened long ago.'

'Very kind indeed.'

'P was in entire agreement.'

'He knew of me?'

'Of course. You are too modest, George.'

Garner shielded his face with his glass of Algerian. 'What are the strings?'

'No strings, George. Very few, anyway. Quarterly magazine, to be called *Light*.'

'*Light*,' said Garner.

'It's not bad, you know,' said Fox defensively. 'Not bad at all. P rather insisted on it, as a matter of fact. And the magazine to be imaginative rather than critical. Non-political, of course. A small editorial board.'

'A board,' said Garner.

'A very small one,' said Fox, and tossed down his Algerian. 'A formality, really. To consist simply of the editor; Sir Theo – if he agrees; P – when he has the time; and me.'

'Sir Theo,' said Garner reflectively, thinking really that here was a concrete instance of Fox's usually mysterious method of achieving literary power without ever writing anything.

'Sir Theo? Oh, a name, you know. As a matter of fact Sir Theo will be most suitable because it's impossible to get him to go anywhere nowadays. Ha ha! He certainly won't interfere. No one will.' Fox filled up Garner's glass with a generous gesture. 'Well, what do you think of it?' His tongue must surely fall out now.

'Very American,' said Garner. 'The financier with a concern for letters. Very American.'

'Industrialist,' corrected Fox, narrowing his eyes like a cat approaching fish.

Garner sighed and laid down his knife and fork. Since he always bolted his food he had now to wait awkwardly while Fox finished his. He made his first truly-felt remark. 'What about money?'

Fox talked. The waiter cleared away. Fox ordered Camembert and Garner a pastry. By the time they were drinking coffee Garner was beginning to imagine himself the editor of *Light*. The money was satisfactory, even generous. It meant that he could give up entirely the drudgery of reviewing. Fox had suggested that Cuffs might do the business side, and so the whole thing could be run from Garner's room at the publishers. Or he could, Garner thought, keep on the reviewing and take out another endowment policy. He had reached the age when the importance of endowment policies outweighed the uncertainty of history.

As they waited on the pavement for a taxi, Fox said: 'Well, I shall tell P you accept, then.'

Garner put on his broad-brimmed black hat. 'I think so.'

'Probably he'll want to see you.'

'P?'

Garner's irony was too subtle. 'P,' said Fox seriously. 'Sorry I can't tell you more. Yes, he'll want to see you.'

'I can stand it,' said Garner.

'I'm so pleased about it all,' said Fox, waving his hand. 'I'm sure that *Light* can play an important part in the literary set-up at the moment. It's not politics or even criticism we want in these hard times but imagination. More imagination.' The taxi drew up to the kerb. 'Can I give you a lift, George?'

'No,' said Garner, pulling his hat further over his eyes. 'No, thank you. Got a call . . .' His voice trailed off and he found himself grasping Fox's damp hand. As the taxi drove off he called: 'Thank you again for remembering me,' but probably too late for Fox to hear. Then mercifully he was quite alone, standing on the pavement's edge, wondering why he had felt a fool in his hat because Fox was not wearing one, and knowing that he would have felt an equal fool if the roles had been reversed. He shambled off.

In Oxford Street he saw a man selling toy mice under the veranda of John Lewis's: the man held his hands in front of his chest and the mouse appeared to run over them. When Garner had doggedly discovered the secret he walked on, thinking of the magazine. In spite of his consciousness of the absurdity of his excitement he started to compose his first editorial. 'Imaginative rather than factual, ethical rather than political; nevertheless this review will have regard for facts and will be keenly interested in the human needs which give rise to politics . . .'

Waiting for the southbound traffic to halt at Oxford Circus, he saw next to him a young man with a scarred face, a fragmentary, consumed ear, a lower eyelid drawn down and showing a crescent of liquid red eye-socket. Garner averted his head quickly. It was, of course, guilt which made him feel so agonizingly the lingering horrors of the War, but the guilt must have an earlier origin than 1939. Since he believed quite implicitly in Freudian motivation he racked his memory, as he had so often done before, for an infantile clue to his present excessive emotion. But, as before, the search was fruitless and his thoughts easily diverted. At Selfridges he was continuing the editorial.

'The central fact of our time is Horror.' He rejected, on reflection, the capital letter. '. . . is horror. The fantasy of the mature Romantics – of Poe, of Beddoes, of Hood – is our reality. *Their* reality distorted their dreams because it repressed their desires. *Our* reality can give us true dreams because our desires are independent of it. The lesson of the death camps is this: that man's spirit . . .' He could not make up his mind whether or not to cross the road and go into Bumpus's. He hovered, schizophrenic, on the pavement, staring through the veils of traffic. And then the decisive thought came that if he resisted buying any books his salary from *Light* would be added to larger wealth. Besides, what was the point of walking home and saving the pennies if on the way he was going to squander shillings? He resolved again, as he had resolved many times, to read nothing but the books he already owned. Really to get to know the Jonson plays; to find quotations from Montaigne rising unbidden to his lips – how inspiring and how economical! He turned and walked with fresh vigour up the slope to Marble Arch.

Garner's flat was in a decayed square off the Bayswater Road. Through the tall windows of his living-room he could see the plane trees of the gardens, their trunks patched like the smooth hide of some animal. In the quiet of the afternoon an old woman tottered round the railings of the square. Above her, two pigeons barged about heavily among the branches.

Before him, on the desk, was a neat pile of quarto sheets. He took out and unscrewed his fountain-pen with the sense of power and pleasure which that action never failed to bring. He wrote his address at the head of the top sheet, and then paused. He emptied the ashtray into the waste-paper basket. He picked his nose unrewardingly and stared out at the trees, the pigeons, and the old woman's tedious progress. He was not composed. Before the scene in front of him floated Fox's face, the long white teeth clenched on Fox's ridiculous meerschaum pipe. Into Garner's mind came fragments of their conversation that, remembering his own contribution to them, made him squirm in an agony of lost opportunity and regret for indiscretions.

He got up and went to the mirror over the fireplace. By the mirror hung a narrow leather pocket which contained a pair of scissors. He took out the scissors and trimmed his beard and moustache. The face he saw in the glass was small for the thick body, its complexion not pale, not ruddy, but rough, like a papiermâché mask: the eyes were grey, the coarse hair the colour of an old penny. As he looked at the face its solemn expression did not change.

He took the feather duster from its hook near the largest bookcase and flicked the whisker clippings off the marble mantelpiece. Then he went to the open bookcases and dusted the books and, tenderly, the rows of box files on a bottom shelf which contained the drafts of his letters and the replies to the originals. He looked at the files with emotion. They were what lifted him out of the Fox class: they surely were his chance, if he had one, of immortality – that two or three hundred years of posterity's affection and understanding. The old happy thought came to him – the thought as absurd as the daydream of snatching a millionaire from under the wheels of a bus, so absurd that even in the privacy of his own mind he passed over it quickly – that he was a sort of Horace Walpole. A negative Horace Walpole, of course – shy, not very well known, ill-educated: in this obscure corner of London adding, year by year, solidly, secretly, to the meticulous record of his partial but serious view of contemporary life. He hung up the feather duster and went back to the desk confident and excited. He took his pen and, in the elegant but affected chancery script he had so laboriously trained his clumsy hand to write, put at the top left of the page the words 'Dear Widgery'.

It was comic in a way. Garner had not seen Widgery for twelve years and might very well never see him again. But Widgery kept (he was sure) all his long letters and answered some. Of the literary world in which Garner, when he moved, moved, Widgery had no first-hand knowledge: he was an engineer in Lancashire. But he was also a gossip: he was old-fashioned, he had leisure. Garner had chosen him as a correspondent very carefully.

And yet there was more in their queer relationship than Garner's calculation and Widgery's amiability. They had been to the same private school – a ramshackle school for the boys of uninterested parents on the Lincolnshire coast. They had not been precisely friends – Widgery was the younger by a couple of years – but in their penultimate year they had been thrown together as, in the school's decline, some of Garner's contemporaries had left in a body. Their desultory letters after leaving had, under Garner's tutelage, blossomed into this monstrous correspondence.

Dear Widgery: Last night Kew recorded the highest April temperature for thirty-two years, but the plane trees in the square are still as naked as antlers. Perhaps they are always naked at this time of year – no one could be more ignorant of such things than I. But this twaddle is only to prove to myself that I can at least delay for two sentences some news of the world of letters which has excited me and which must now bore you.

I am to be £400 a year the richer for a little, not-unpleasurable work – through the machinations of Roderick Fox, poetaster, literary politician, Harrovian . . .

When Garner thought of Widgery he thought of a tall diffident boy and not of the taller, heavily-moustached man into whom the boy had grown. It was to the boy – receptive, silent, amusing when at ease – that the letters were written. And, oddly enough, boy's letters came back – thin, facetious, charming. Widgery had never really enlarged, through the years, the miniature world which his letters presented. His older sister, Viola, who kept house for him; the Victorian villa plumped down in the dingy agricultural plain which surrounded the manufacturing town where Widgery worked; the manager; the operatives – Widgery described these comic surfaces with no hint of any depths his own life might have. He was the most satisfactory of Garner's correspondents.

. . . we had no brandy. The bill for lunch would naturally go to P, one imagines, and Fox would be at least a pound in pocket if one remembers, too, that the wine was Algerian. That was how

Fox's father, a man who sold boots to the armies of 1914-18, made his pile. I await, through Fox, an appointment with P.

And so I came back to the plane trees and the plain paper. The paper – or, rather, three sheets of it – must be covered today. I still don't know quite how. That is why I had to write to you before I started. The writer's main problem is how to compose himself – but not so as to eradicate *all* his restlessness, otherwise he will be too pessimistic about his art to bring himself to write at all. I resisted telling Fox what I was working on – that was my only triumph today – though the temptation to blurt it out and spoil everything was very great. All human temptation is the offer of a few moments' godlike warmth and excitement at the price of hours of self-disgust. I can safely tell you everything because you aren't interested.

I looked for a letter from you as I came in – the letter I have looked for during the last three weeks. Have you taken the influenza, which I suppose still lingers in such bleak pockets as Askington? . . .

As Garner wrote his letter his attention gradually floated away from it and attached itself to the complications and descriptions in the novel he was writing. Half mechanically he shaped his phrases for Widgery while with a growing assurance he perceived the richness of those complications and descriptions – perceived how they might be taken further to the completeness which would prove only a source of fresh development. The actual words of the sentence which would bridge the hitherto daunting gap between the novel so far and the new relations in his head shaped itself on his lips. Without haste he put the letter on one side and drew out a fresh sheet of paper.

Chapter Two

THE old couple in the flat above started dropping their boots on the floor. From the yard at the back came crescendo wailing as one or other of the ground-floor children was thwarted or ignored. It was morning.

Garner put out his hand and pressed the switch of the bedside lamp. There was no answering light. He joggled the switch several times without result. He heaved himself out of bed, groped to the curtains, and drew them back to reveal a newspaper-coloured day. He went to the memorandum pad on the mantelpiece and wrote on it 'Fri. Buy 60-watt bulb.' Then he looked at his face in the mirror and took the crumbs of sleep out of his eyes. He repeated some lines of a poem he had read in the night:

> To tickle the maggot born in an empty head,
> And wheedle a world that loves him not,
> For it is but a world of the dead.

But he had slept – he calculated – five hours: slept well. That gave him a sense of power. The image in the mirror winked at him without smiling. He donned his dressing-gown and went into the tiny kitchen to put the kettle on. As he descended the stairs for the post he thought of the magazine and that there might be a letter from Fox or even P. In the hall he encountered one of the ground-floor children who was just too frightened by his beard and tousled hair to be rude.

Over his breakfast of tinned pilchards in tomato sauce he read his letters with increasing depression. The green wrapper from the agency contained two cuttings. One was his article on Wilkie Collins: he read it again rapidly but with great enjoyment. That was fine. But the other cutting was an extract from a survey of fiction in one of the lesser weeklies by a man he had never heard of. He was dealt with in a sentence: 'Nothing has been heard of Mr George Garner since he went into the MOI (or was it the BBC) during the war: judging by *Goats and Compasses* this is less of a calamity than one would have thought ten years ago.'

Garner's heart beat faster. It was absurd, but even such illiterate criticism upset him. He pushed the unfinished pilchards away and got *Goats and Compasses* from the shelf. He opened it at random and read. His heart quietened. The prose was rich, the observation was keen, the grasp competent. The unknown fiction surveyor must be mad. He closed the book and skimmed through the Collins article again. He poured himself another cup of molasses-hued tea, lit a Woodbine, and looked out at the grey clouds slowly changing their chalky outlines over the still trees in the square. Utterly mad. He thought of his good sleep, then of his solid war-time work at the Ministry of Information, and finally of the sheets of his new novel piling thickly on his desk. How could it possibly be said that he was a backnumber? He reached for the memorandum pad and wrote: 'Loneliness of failure: loneliness of success.'

Then he opened a letter and read with a different unease.

Brick House,
Bell,
Nr Askington,
Thursday

Dear Mr Garner: William often speaks to me of you, and I am sure that when he writes to you he sometimes mentions my name.

18

We actually met many years ago but you may not remember that. I feel that you are not only a friend of William's but of the family, and that must be the excuse for inflicting our troubles on you. We lead a very quiet life here and I really do not think there is anyone to whom I can turn except you. I know that you must have a tender place for William. I wondered at first whether perhaps William had not come to London and was staying with you or at least had called on you, but now that is a very slender hope. The fact is, Mr Garner, William has left Brick House without a word to anyone. I took the liberty of opening your last letter to him in case there was in it some clue to his whereabouts, but I saw from it that you, too, were wondering why there had been no word. Nothing like this has ever happened before and I am beginning to be desperately worried.

If there is anything I can do that you can suggest from your great knowledge of William I shall be deeply grateful. If by any chance you should be able to spare the time there is always a bed for you here.

Sincerely yours,
Viola Widgery

P.S. Of course, there is much that cannot be said in a letter.

When Garner had read the letter twice he stubbed out his cigarette on a fragment of pilchard and immediately lit another – that was his ration gone for the whole morning. But it was monstrous! He had no 'great knowledge' of William Widgery. It was unfair and wrong for his sister to have written. He stared at the box files of his correspondence as though each one, like the Widgery file, contained a time-bomb which would blow sky high the defences round his life, admitting boredom, responsibilities, anxiety. His mind was already forming the phrases of a letter to Miss Widgery – phrases of frigidity, denial, alibis.

He read absently the remainder of his post: there was no

letter from Fox. He picked up the newspaper but super-imposed on the headlines of stupidity and hatred were Miss Widgery's insipid and assuming sentences. He prepared for the short morning stroll which he always employed for meditation on his work – prepared for it not with the usual enjoyable anticipation but with irritation and worry as though a dental appointment lay just beyond it.

As he was tying his shoes there was a knock on the door. When he opened it the eldest girl of the downstairs family was standing there. This was the girl who tidied his flat. His look of exasperation faded because it was useless.

'Good morning,' he said. 'I'm afraid I'm late today, Marjorie.'

The girl put the key, which she was going to use had he been out, into the pocket of her overall, and slipped past him straight to the rumpled bed. She began deftly to put it in order. He shut the door and stood watching her.

'I'm going out in five minutes,' he said, feeling as he always did at his rare encounters with her a compulsion to talk a great deal, to account for his actions. 'So I shan't disturb you for long.'

'You aren't disturbing me,' she said, looking neither at him nor the bed.

'I'm upset this morning,' he said. The luxury of confession made him feel almost happy.

'Has the story gone wrong?' she asked, remembering other conversations.

'No,' said Garner. 'Something else – too complicated to worry you about. In my middle age I can't bear to have my routine destroyed.'

'I only wish someone would destroy *my* routine.'

'Poor Marjorie,' Garner said. She pronounced it rou'ine:

he must remember that for the proletarian character in his novel. He watched the movements of her hands, thinking of something else to say to her.

'Did you finish *The Old Curiosity Shop*?' he asked.

'Oh, a long time ago.'

'What are you reading now?'

'Rubbish. There's an awful lot of rubbish in the library.'

'Why didn't you go on with Dickens?'

'I want to read modern stories – about things that happen now. But I don't know how to choose the good ones. Perhaps the good ones aren't in the library.'

'There aren't many good ones,' Garner said.

'They aren't truthful,' she said.

'You must ask them to translate – or whatever you call it – mine,' said Garner. 'Only mine aren't truthful either.'

'I bet they are,' she said, putting the cover neatly on the divan. He suddenly realized the extent of her skill.

'Who taught you how to make beds?' he asked.

'They learned us at school,' she said, on her careful but unfaltering way to the table.

'Was everyone as good as you?'

'Most of the girls were better than me. I wasn't interested in all that. I wanted to be a typist.'

'Why couldn't you be a typist?'

'Wasn't clever enough.'

'It seems to me *all* sightless people have to make an extraordinary effort if they're going to live at all.' He used the word he had heard her use.

'Everyone could do it if they were sightless.'

'Do you really think so?'

'Certain,' she said, and took a pile of crockery to the kitchen.

'We all ought to be blind, then,' he muttered, getting his hat and the memorandum pad. 'I'm going now,' he called to the girl. 'Good-bye.'

On the way downstairs he read the notes on the pad. *Buy 60-watt bulb.*

He did not go back to his flat that morning. As he walked along the Bayswater Road he found himself unable to sink into a comfortable complex of thought about his book. His rou'ine was certainly disturbed.

He took a bus to Piccadilly Circus and walked up Shaftesbury Avenue towards all those places which usually had power to console him. Past the theatres he turned into Soho and found an electrician's where he bought his bulb. Then he looked through some records in Harridge's second-hand shop, hesitating over Bartok's Music for Strings, Percussion, and Celesta, lighting yet another cigarette as the titles warmed his interest. Standing on the pavement outside, having bought nothing, he threw away the butt of the cigarette and with it the warmth.

The sun came out and shone crudely on the milk bars and rubber shops of Cambridge Circus. Garner made for the colour of the art books in Zwemmer's corner window. What, he thought, if the wretched critic were right for the wrong reasons? There was certainly something suspicious in the way he gravitated towards the records and the books – solitary pleasures, drugs, escapes. All right for a poet, but the novelist should be in neither Bayswater nor the Charing Cross Road, but Lewisham – or Askington. When he considered his novel analytically he saw that it concerned himself, not other people. And when he surveyed the circle of his acquaintance he saw that there were no friends among it, and, indeed, only one person he ever met with any pleasure and spoke to with relaxation – a blind girl who did his chores. He asked himself, with a strange feeling of detachment, whether any of them liked him: strange, because not for years had he experienced the luxury of knowing himself cared for. That part of his feelings, he suddenly realized, had shrivelled away with disuse, and in its place was an elaborate system of ersatz and lonely enjoyment – the music of the gramophone, evenings of intense reading, the breakfast tins of pilchards and sardines.

And as he stood by the window of the shop which displayed ranks of nude photographs, a simple, foolish yearning came over him, as though he were a child again. It almost brought tears to his eyes. Beyond the dramatically shadowed navels and solid breasts, a memory rose of the dining-room at school. The most junior boy at each table had to transport the plates of food for the boys at his table from the masters' table where it was served. A pale, slim, new boy, carrying two plates of rather desiccated ginger pudding, inadvertently allowed the contents of one of them to slip to the linoleumed floor. He stood petrified amid the juvenile cries of derision and the master's irritated sarcasm, his eyes glistening; and Garner, himself not long promoted from the office of food monitor, knew instinctively how the boy was longing to be back at home, longing for the embracing kindness and understanding of his mother. Of course, the boy was Widgery.

Garner turned into Collet's bookshop. Before he looked round his eyes scanned the fiction and lit reassuringly on the cheap edition of *Goats and Compasses*. The new pattern of his day began to form itself, already more bearable because more choate. He would fritter the morning away in the resigned, comforted mood of the losing gambler who sees and sets a disastrous but firm limit to his losses. In the afternoon he had already arranged to go into Cuffs. In the evening a choice of distractions presented themselves, almost evil in their suggestion of pleasure after a day of nonwork: two Mozart piano concertos at the Wigmore Hall, *Duck Soup* at the Academy, *The Duchess of Malfi* at the Old Vic. He would bask in the evil, forgetting his novel, Widgery, and the new-found sense of his personal deficiencies.

He came out of Collet's, turned into Newport Street, and then down St Martin's Lane. It was half past eleven, so he went into the pub on the corner of St Martin's Court and ordered a pint of mild. He glowered at it, still wearing his big black hat, the bulb bulging the pocket of his hairy tweed jacket, his beard sunk into his woollen tie. Foolishly he thought that some discerning occupant of the saloon bar might be whispering to a companion: 'George Garner, the novelist'; and then recognized his folly by smiling wryly and opening his copy of the midday *Star*. All the same, he continued to act his part a little.

Cuffs, the publishers, were in Long Acre – a mock-Regency façade with bow windows displaying the firm's publications, and a rabbit warren of rooms behind. Right at the back, on the third floor, was the small room set aside for Garner. It contained a table, two chairs, and an old bookcase like a provincial town hall. On the table were piles of manuscripts, paper-bound page proofs, a telephone, and a thick notebook which Garner used for his reflections while looking out at the view from the window – the white tiled walls of the air shaft. Through the ventilators of a glassed-in room on the floor below came the irregular clatter of typewriters.

Garner sat at the table, somnolent after his lunch of beer and sausage rolls. In front of him lay the manuscript of the frightful autobiography of a dashing Rear Admiral which Cuffs had commissioned him to rewrite.

'At the beginning of April [Garner read] Jerry was appointed DDNAS. The usual remarks were made. But Jerry was no fool. He knew the requirements of the fighting man in the Far East and was fully determined to ensure that those requirements were met henceforth . . .'

How could one rewrite that? He pushed the autobiography away to wait a more inspired occasion, and pulled towards him the manuscript of a novel called *All Are Lovers*. Could it happily be dismissed out of hand as tripe? He opened it in the middle and took a test reading.

'She tensed her body so that his encircling arms should not discover the inward sobbing that she felt must surely be shaking her. Her life before her was a blank, glaring sheet – a cinema screen whose film had broken and was whirling senselessly round in the projector. "Darling Carol," he was saying, "Darling Carol".'

Garner sighed. He would have to start at the beginning: it bore some, certainly, of the marks of a Cuffs notable first novel.

The telephone rang. 'Good afternoon, Mr Garner,' said the too-cultured voice of Miss Cherry, the telephonist. 'Mr Alastair wished to know if you were in this afternoon and if so could you spare him a few minutes?'

'Yes,' said Garner, his voice inaudible through phlegm.

He cleared his throat. 'Yes, certainly.' Then he added: 'Shall I go and see him now?' But the voice of Miss Cherry had cut itself off.

While Garner still sat in a state of indecision, wondering whether to make a move or await events, Alastair Cuff came in discreetly at the door. He was a tall man in his early thirties who in the street wore a smart bowler hat pressed down over his eyes, which concealed the fact of his premature baldness: indoors, tufts of honey-coloured hair stood out startlingly over his ears. He had been, during the war, a very young infantry colonel, and had returned, with ideas, to a directorship in the family company. Garner was always uneasy with him, fearing his drive, envying his poise, despising his command over and acceptance of mundane affairs.

'Hello, Garner. May I sit down?' Alastair Cuff settled himself on the second chair, disposing gracefully of the ample folds of his unbuttoned clerical grey double-breasted jacket. 'I had Roderick Fox on the telephone this morning.'

'Ah,' said Garner.

'About this periodical called *Light*.' Cuff offered his gold cigarette case: Garner declined with a shake of his head. 'Is there really anything in it?'

'Aperiently, said Mrs Gamp.' Garner's embarrassment took the form of facetiousness.

'Well then,' said Cuff, 'I'm awfully pleased about it for your sake. Of course, with you as editor we'll be glad to look after things. Prestige and all that.'

'Afraid there'll not be much more than prestige in it for you,' mumbled Garner.

'No,' said Cuff, rather coolly. 'But Jimmy Foster can

take it on his plate without making a meal of it – with the house organ, you know.'

'Oh yes, I've had dealings with Jimmy.' Cuff always referred to the firm's glorified list as 'the house organ': it was called *Off the Cuff*, a name the firm's founder thought wildly go-ahead in the 1880s.

'Talking about the house organ, will you do a piece on the Meredith omnibus for it?'

'I've done it,' said Garner.

'Good Lord, did I ask you before?'

'No, your uncle.'

'We must really get some terms of reference out for the directors of this firm,' said Cuff, half seriously. 'The Meredith isn't HL's cup of tea at all. Sorry about that.' And then, to Garner's consternation, Cuff fixed him with a look of concern. 'I hope you don't mind my asking, Garner, but are you quite fit these days?'

'Eh?' said Garner. 'Fit? Yes, I'm fine. Fine.'

'You had that bout of tonsillitis –'

'That was ages ago.'

Cuff said: 'I felt at the time that we ought to have done something. Laid on a nurse – that sort of caper. But I kept putting it off, until it was too late. You live alone, don't you?'

Garner's alarm grew, for he saw in Cuff's look and behind his casual words a genuine feeling – he saw pity, the pity one has for someone with an incurable deformity. And in the light of Cuff's feeling Garner for an instant perceived himself with the eyes of percipient others – his situation, personality, life. What he saw frightened him.

'Yes, I've lived alone for years,' said Garner, with the false calm of one who has found a formula for an awkward predicament.

'It must have its advantages,' said Cuff. 'But you're too useful a slave for us to neglect.'

Garner laughed with relief at the lowered tone. 'I have a very good char,' he said. 'The man in London with a good char is a man whose life is basically contented.' And as though it were a secret he thought of the pupils of Marjorie's eyes as she spoke to him, as undifferentiated as a dog's, roaming about in enormous spaces over his head.

'All the same,' said Alastair Cuff, 'you need a bit of home cooking now and then. You must come and have dinner with us one night.'

'I'd love to,' said Garner, without the slightest intention of ever doing so.

Cuff leaned forward and stubbed out his cigarette in the ashtray. Garner saw the light gleam on his pink skull and thought how he had always misjudged him, that behind his keen, merciless air was a kindliness verging on sentimentality.

'Why don't you come tomorrow night?' asked Cuff.

Words rushed almost involuntarily to Garner's lips, but when they were out he saw that they had been inevitable and he felt the sensitiveness and well-being of one who after long and painful anxiety confesses his secret trouble, weeps, and is forgiven. 'I'm awfully sorry,' he said, 'but I have to go up north tomorrow. I shall be away a day or two – hope the firm won't mind. One of my dearest friends' – Cuff's sympathy permitted him to use words he had never used before, words that might have come from the manuscripts on the table – 'has asked me to go to see him. Some frightful family trouble that demands the old family friend.'

And as he boasted about Widgery the actual man took

28

urgent shape in his mind and he knew that he really would go to Askington, that Widgery's well-being mattered to him, that his responsibilities extended beyond those two Bayswater rooms with their pile of quarto paper.

Chapter Three

ALL the same as the train drew out of Euston between the grey walls of banking and tall houses, Garner felt a strong sense of the unreality of the situation. *Our Mutual Friend* lay open on his knee, the usual middle-aged spinster, the usual fat man, the usual Army NCO, were disposed about the compartment – he might have been making a journey for a commonplace purpose. But the first movement of the train had severed the cord that linked him with his normal activities, and the background to his being had become empty and light, as though a death had suddenly changed his life.

He felt in his pocket for his cigarettes and found an unfamiliar piece of paper. When he opened it he saw that it was the draft of his telegram to Miss Widgery. 'Will come after lunch tomorrow – Garner.' Following the word 'tomorrow' were several phrases which he had added in turn and then rejected – such as 'Will return same day' and 'Regards' – which betrayed some of his emotions about it all.

He watched the patterns on the banking and permanent way which the sun made breaking between houses, and felt himself acting the part of the detached but sympathetic person who smoothes away anxiety. He imagined himself patting Viola Widgery's shoulder, suggesting sensible courses of action, and finally talking to the tracked-down Widgery himself in tones of infinite understanding. And then moving softly away from Askington, out of the Widgerys' lives, like the Stranger in *The Passing of the Third Floor Back*, leaving them changed and serene.

Really, he thought, finding his cigarettes at last and lighting one, he had no character at all – not like the fat man in the opposite corner, who having made an amorphous limpness of the *Daily Mirror* was now cleaning his ears with a paper clip, even his navy serge suit moulded monolithically to his ego. But Garner simply reflected whoever encountered him. Like Proteus, he was difficult of access: when consulted he refused, by assuming different shapes, to give answers, and eluded people's grasp by taking savage forms or forms which simply disappeared. The solid figure with the beard and the apparatus of books, periodicals, notebook, and pencil (which the fat man saw, and no doubt placed in a specific and probably inferior category) did not exist for Garner and did not really exist for anyone else. But perhaps (Garner went on to think) the character of the fat man was to its owner equally illusory.

In that case (Garner turned back to the book on his knee) what was Dickens up to? Was a novelist no more than the great mirror on the Veneerings' sideboard? 'Reflects Mrs Podsnap . . . quantity of bone, neck and nostrils like a rocking horse . . . Reflects charming old Lady Tippins . . . with an immense obtuse drab oblong face, like a face in a table spoon . . .' Yes, indeed, how right Dickens was! And Chekhov, too, who reflected the inconsequence of action as Dickens the inconsequence of appearance. To go deeper was to bog oneself down in illusion – the illusion of sentimentality and of intellectualism.

The train passed suburban playing-fields and little parks, where, on this Saturday morning, the brightly coloured midget figures of boys ran about in the predetermined patterns of football. A belt of trees appeared, a canal with green banks, a raw rim of partially-built red-brick houses, the road ran up a hump bridge over the canal, a tradesman's van was halted at a cottage with an intensely cultivated garden, the light green of meadows moved past the window and past the dark ploughed fields behind them, a farm trailed its smoke in the distance – they were out of London.

What shall I do when I get to Askington? thought Garner. As always when he faced something unusual, he tried to make the improbable real by imagining it. First he would catch the bus to Bell – the single-decker bus with its load of factory workers and housewives which had so often featured in Widgery's wartime letters when his car had been laid up for lack of petrol. He tried to visualize the stop outside Widgery's house, the rhododendron-lined drive up to the front door, the conservatory at the side, Miss Widgery's welcome – and then his power to see anything plausible failed. But he comforted himself with the thought that whatever happens to oneself, however extraordinary or painful, becomes eventually commonplace and bearable. The empire of self constantly added to itself new wild tracts of territory which it was able to drain, plough, populate, and thus become once again an ordered, homogeneous entity.

The bus-stop of his imagination proved a poor approximation to reality. Garner descended from the single-decker, almost empty at that dead hour of the afternoon, dangling his canvas hold-all, and found himself in front of a black brick public-house, with its window copings and threshold bright with hearthstone. This was the Bell Arms. Next to it was a shed with a board over it which said 'James Forshaw and Sons. Funeral Directors.' Some children came along eating ice-cream blocks out of unmanageable paper wrappers.

'Can you tell me where Brick House is?' Garner asked politely. They stared at his beard and hat as though he had been a Chinese. The eldest girl shook her head. 'Mr Widgery's house,' pursued Garner.

Light dawned on the girl. 'It's over yonder,' she said, pointing down the road where a blue slate roof topped some still-bare trees. Garner thanked her and blundered off. The children turned round to watch him, drops of forgotten ice-cream falling on their shoes.

The imagined drive was curiously foreshortened, the house smaller. And as, to gain time, he carefully shut the gate, he found that he was not thinking of the strangeness of the experience at all but of the discomfort of his grubby hands and greasy face, and about the little girl's archaic use of 'yonder'. The bell was a knob which promoted a delayed, shaking ring in the recesses of the house. It summoned a middle-aged domestic with frizzy hair, a squint, and a white apron. This person said: 'Good *aff*ternoon, Mr Garner. Come in, won't you?' And took his things. How fatally expected he was.

He was ushered straight into a sitting-room which looked on to the lawn at the back and a quantity of blackish evergreens. The easy chairs and sofa were covered in the same washed-out chintz of the curtains. Some dark landscapes in broad gilt frames broke the whiteness of the walls: books broke the whiteness of the low bookshelves round the fireplace in which the glow of a fire marked the two hundred miles north of Garner's journey. Viola Widgery stood in the middle of the room, tall like her brother, with grey hair but black, arched eyebrows.

She said: 'Mr Garner, it's very kind indeed of you to have come.'

'No,' he said. 'No, not at all.'

She invited him to sit down on the chintz: he felt his thick tweed suit as out of place on it as a labourer in a first-class compartment.

'I expect,' she said, 'all your plans have been upset –'

He started talking quickly: 'No, indeed. I never have any plans. I live alone, you know. I read for a publisher and that means I'm not tied to an office. I carry my work about with me, really.' He laughed, beginning to feel absurdly as though the whole thing might pass off in chit-chat, without mentioning Widgery at all.

'All the same,' she said, 'it is a very long way.'

'The 9.47 is a very good train.'

'Yes, isn't it? Though I haven't travelled on it for many years. I haven't been in London since before the war.'

'You'd find it much changed,' said Garner, trying, like a child with a bad school report, to keep the conversation off the dangerous topic. He watched Viola Widgery's hands, clasped in the lap of her navy-blue dress. There was a momentary silence into which he felt Widgery's disappearance would certainly have broken but for the entry of the cross-eyed maid with a tray of tea. The silence did not come again until Miss Widgery had poured and Garner had eaten a sandwich and praised the fruit cake. The clasped hands unclasped themselves and were transferred, trembling slightly, to the arms of the easy chair.

'I still haven't heard from William,' said Miss Widgery.

Garner shifted his body and gazed out of the window. Clearly, he would never pat Miss Widgery on the shoulder. 'How long is it now?' he asked, gently.

'Three weeks.'

'And he left without a word.'

'Without a word.'

'Haven't the police been able to discover anything?'

'I haven't been to the police.'

'Oh,' said Garner.

'You corresponded regularly with William, Mr Garner, but I don't think you knew him intimately.'

'In his letters he told me a great deal about his life – his work, friends, this house.'

'Did he ever mention someone called Philip Rogers?'

'I don't remember the name,' said Garner.

'Of course,' said Miss Widgery, 'there is a large part of everybody's life which remains for the most part underneath the surface, which only shows itself during a great disturbance.' Garner was startled into bringing his gaze out of the garden into Viola Widgery's eyes, which were pale blue under the arched black brows. 'As a novelist that is a commonplace to you.'

'Yes,' said Garner, wondering not about Widgery but his sister, whether there could possibly be any depths in her milieu to accommodate a submerged life of any substantial bulk.

As though she had read his thoughts, she went on: 'In this small place, where both William and I have lived almost all our lives, we present a very ordinary surface of our characters to our neighbours and acquaintances. I know William would not want me to go to the police.'

Garner waited for the point to be reached, but Miss Widgery stretched out for a silver box and offered him a cigarette. She took one herself, and when he held the flame of his lighter to it he saw that she handled it inexpertly, and knew that for her cigarettes were a concomitant only of crises. He made his effort. 'There's something – ah, disgraceful that Widger – that William has done?'

As soon as the words were out of his mouth he thought that perhaps he had gone too far. The brown, varnished landscapes, the wool tapestry firescreen, cried out their evidence of generations of Lancashire virtue and industry. How could Widgery possibly have defrauded his friends or got the farmer's daughter in the family way?

But Garner's words seemed to break for Miss Widgery the barrier of convention that had been between them as soon as Garner, like a polite afternoon caller, had pulled the bell – as though she had hinted at the worst and could now easily reveal it to be not quite the worst. She pulled the cigarette out of her mouth with a violence that suggested it had been glued there. 'No,' she said. 'No. But William is different from –' She did not complete the comparison but took another pull at the cigarette and then exuded a great cloud of smoke. 'About six weeks ago,' she said, 'William engaged a young man at the mill. He was new to Askington: he came from London. He was called Philip Rogers. He wasn't a mill-hand, you know. In fact he was quite cultured, and when he came here he used to talk to William about books.'

Garner said: 'He came here?'

'Oh yes, quite often. William soon made a friend of him. Mr Rogers was very good-looking. I always think of William saying to me after he had been to supper for the first time: "Rogers reminds me of my youth. Do you remember that school story that was serialized in the BOP? The hero always used to be tossing back his lemon-coloured

36

hair. Or perhaps it was the hero's best friend. And it may have been a serial in *Chums*."'

'That sounds very like your brother,' said Garner, smiling.

Viola Widgery nodded. ''Mr Rogers' hair was lemon-coloured. He was very polite and very deferential to William. I think, too, he was useful to William in some way at the mill. I disliked him very much.'

She got rid of her cigarette with evident relief.

'Yes,' she said, 'I disliked him. I don't think I was jealous of him. William may have told you in his letters that I am interested in criminology – in an amateurish way, you know. For no reason really Mr Rogers reminded me of one of those figures who turn up on criminal charges from time to time – those men who seem to charm some people and repulse others. They often have a smattering of culture – George Joseph Smith played the organ, you remember. But to anyone who could look at them without bias they must always have seemed to be acting a part – just *too* agreeable, *too* accommodating, not able to cover quite plausibly enough their lack of moral fibre. And with a sort of gap in their history where their previous misdeeds were. I'm really not exaggerating the impression Mr Rogers made on me.'

By now Garner was fairly hanging on her words. In Widgery's letters Viola had appeared as a slightly comic person interested in the potting of shrimps, the counting of bed-linen, punctuality at meals, and the weeding of borders. If Widgery had been as perfunctory about his own character as about his sister's, clearly Garner knew next to nothing about him. It was the old point of the Dickensian view of people.

'Sometimes,' Miss Widgery was saying, 'I thought that Mr Rogers was out to get money from William. He hadn't a very good job at the mill. But he ran a car, he was always well dressed – in an artistic sort of way.'

Garner crossed his gingerbread-tweed legs self-consciously.

'I think William did give him money,' said Miss Widgery. 'But that aspect of it all proved to be unimportant.' Her voice deepened with suppressed feeling. 'You'll remember William as he was at school, Mr Garner. Very sensitive and shy. He was brought up in a family of girls. We have two older sisters who are married. My father died when we were all quite young. I realize now how bad all these circumstances were for William. He has never married, as you know.'

'Yes, I see,' said Garner, who felt as though he had been given the key to a code which ran through the long series of Widgery's letters to him – an easy code which he had been a simpleton not to have guessed from the start.

'Before Mr Rogers came to Askington,' said Viola Widgery, with more confidence now that she had at last made her point, 'we frequently had a crowd of young people to supper on Saturday and Sunday evenings. But he seemed to make all William's friends vanish. There is safety in numbers.'

Garner could hardly credit the crowds of young people: Widgery's letters had been so conspicuous by the absence of such provincial frivolity. He found that his mouth had been open, and closed it.

'William deeply admires youth, for its own sake,' she continued. 'I expect he often told you how he hated becoming middle-aged.' She laughed fondly. 'He's become very bald lately. Sometimes, when the young men were here, he used to wear his cap in the house, making ridiculous excuses for it. All that ended with Mr Rogers. With him William wasn't flippant. One week-end they went walking in the Lakes. Another they went to Manchester to see a play and hear the Hallé. But I know that William wasn't happy. He lost a lot of weight: he had no appetite. When they came in one night after I'd gone to bed William was so long coming up that I went out on the landing, and heard him down below weeping.'

She had long stopped looking at Garner. To relieve the tension he went to the window and lit another cigarette. Behind him he heard her say: 'It is terrible to have to tell you this. But you are the only person I could possibly tell – who could understand what it was all about. And understand the real feeling behind it.'

A fresh weight of responsibility descended upon him and he felt more inadequate than ever.

She said: 'Now you can guess what has happened. I reproach myself bitterly. I never spoke to William about Mr Rogers. I'm sure he thought that I didn't know what was going on. And so when his feelings forced him away he left no word. I thought he would be back in a matter of days, but the days have gone by and turned into weeks.'

There was a silence. Garner turned round and said: 'Don't reproach yourself. I don't think you could have changed things.' He was moved. 'You think he has run away with Rogers, thrown everything up?'

Her voice wavered. 'Or followed him – run after him.'

'Yes,' said Garner, 'of course.' He looked helplessly at the cigarette-box, at the tea-things over which a wave of untidiness had passed. He said: 'Now what can I do, Miss Widgery?'

She looked at him almost as though he had been a child asking to be amused. He put on a bogus practical air. 'There's the London Telephone Directory – I think you said Rogers had come from London. A personal column advertisement.' His imagination failed. 'And the police. I can't help thinking that you – we – ought to consult the police. They can be very discreet.'

'It will have to be the police in the end.'

Garner tried his best. 'Miss Widgery, I'm sure there is no need to worry too much about William. These – things don't last, you know. He'll come back – unchanged – as though it had never happened.'

For a moment she looked eagerly as though she believed him, and then returned to her sad, fragile composure. 'I know William so well. He could not see Mr Rogers as I could and that makes me afraid.'

Garner refrained from asking 'of what?' They were already too near melodrama for his liking. Had he been brought all this way to riffle through the Rs of the telephone directory and call at W. H. Smith's to place an advertisement?

Viola Widgery said: 'I wonder if you would be kind enough to see Mr Kershaw, the secretary at the mill?'

'Yes, of course,' said Garner, in the dark but glad to be asked to do something that seemed rational.

'I'm sure he knew Mr Rogers better than I. And, of course, he knows that William has gone.'

'He does?'

'I've been very cowardly. I haven't discussed it frankly with him. He knows though – or guesses – roughly what's happened, I'm sure. Unfortunately he won't be at the mill now, being Saturday afternoon.' Garner had a frightful vision of being in Askington until Monday. But Miss Widgery continued: 'He will be at the Town Hall tonight. He produces the Askington Thespians and they are giving a play there. I have two tickets. You could talk to him afterwards, if you would.'

'Yes, of course,' Garner said again. The melodrama had changed to farce.

The curtains drew back on the last scene of Act 3 of *The Years Between*. Diana, a very refined girl, sat on the sofa. Michael, the returned and disillusioned war hero, stood on a pair of steps: he was a plump young man whose hair had been powdered at the temples to denote strain. Robin (the playwright's choice of names was unerring), his much-applauded son of ten, was handing up books to him. Sir Ernest Foster watched warily: he had to battle with a Lancashire accent and a monocle in his portrayal of an intellectual Tory politician. There was some literary talk.

'Did you ever', asked the powdered young man, 'see *Mary Rose*, Ernest?'

Sir Ernest tapped his monocle on the knuckles of his left hand, as he had been doing all evening. 'Did I not!' he exclaimed, in his vibrant voice. 'Cried my eyes out. Had to be supported from the theatre.' He said 'theertur'.

Michael became intense. His words were a commentary on his own situation. 'She came back after twenty years, didn't she? But she never did find what she had lost.'

'What did she do?' piped the boy, in his flat tones.

Michael looked out into the depths of the Town Hall. 'She died, Robin – and her pale ghost haunted the shadows

41

. . .' He gave the twisted smile which indicated his war-twisted soul.

Garner and Miss Widgery sat together in the third row. They could see where the actors' make-up ended and their pale necks began. They tried to find comfort by hoisting their hams to the back of the seats of the bentwood chairs, but the chairs' design had long ceased to afford them any comfort. They had finished Miss Widgery's bag of peppermint creams. At first, Garner had been curiously interested: some of the players were comically bad and he had not seen a successful West End play for years. He was astonished to find how much nonsense it was, to discover the extent of the falsity of its values, and how eagerly its clichés were accepted by the audience - in point of fact, judging by the remarks at the interval, the audience imagined itself to be at a very serious play indeed. He toyed with the idea of an essay on popular 'serious' art - *The Years Between* and the Warsaw Concerto - how it emerged from popular art *simpliciter* and shaded into the plays of Terence Rattigan and the music of Rachmaninov. But finally Garner had been bored - bored to yawning imbecility and fidgets.

On the stage Michael was left alone. He executed his bit of business - looked round the room with the stooping glare that meant deep feeling, fingered lovingly one of his books and then a hideous vase - and eventually called 'Venning! Venning!'

Venning, his barman, entered. This was Kershaw, the producer, secretary of Widgery's company - a slight, gingerish man with indeterminate features. The tiny part of Venning afforded him the opportunity of stealing all the scenes in which he appeared. He now had three lines, each consisting of the one word 'Sir?', which got him three laughs as he played them each with a distinct emotional tone. Garner sighed again at the thought of the ordeal of meeting him.

The scene ground on. Someone backstage put on the record of the church bells playing a victory peal – and then turned down the volume in a hurry. The old Nanny switched on the radio. With masterly effect the last notes of Big Ben were heard. The announcer's voice said, in a Lancashire accent, 'This is London. His Majesty King George the Sixth.' The curtains surmounted their last crisis and creaked across with scarcely a halt.

Garner joined in the applause, turning to Viola Widgery with one of the bogus remarks he had been using all evening. The actors bowed. The effects man took his record of Big Ben off the turntable and substituted the National Anthem. The audience rose and then began to disperse. Garner and Miss Widgery were left standing awkwardly between the bentwood chairs. They started to edge slowly to one of the doors at the side of the stage.

'When I've introduced you to Mr Kershaw,' she said haltingly, 'I'll leave you. I think it would be better for you to have your little talk alone. There is a café on the opposite side of the square. I'll go there and you can come to me afterwards. Perhaps Mr Kershaw would join us if he isn't too busy.'

Behind the scenes the lath and canvas panelling of the Library at the Old Manor was being removed to reveal a vast mahogany organ. A woman carried the hideous vase carefully across the stage. A reporter from the local paper was asking questions of the flushed young boy who had played Robin. Frank Kershaw stood talking in the wings, leaning against the frayed silk which covered the back of an old upright piano. When he saw Garner and Viola Widgery he came towards them. Garner was introduced. 'A splendid performance,' he said firmly.

'They're not a bad lot,' said Kershaw fondly. 'Evie was better than ever, don't you think, Miss Widgery? The *Manchester Guardian* critic was out front: we're all looking forward to seeing what he has to say about her.' Kershaw's broad tones as Venning lay buried beneath a very precise and distinct articulation. Out of the large collar of his battledress blouse came a rather stringy neck: the whites of his blue eyes were slightly bloodshot. He was older than he looked at first glance.

When Miss Widgery at last announced her intention of repairing to the café, it was plain that Kershaw knew what was expected of him. 'Come along to the dressing-room,' he said to Garner. 'It should be getting a bit clearer in there now.'

Garner experienced a pang as Viola Widgery departed: he felt himself launched on an unwished voyage, without maps. The men's dressing-room was grey with smoke. Two tarnished tea-urns reposed in one corner: across them leaned an oak lectern. Some beer bottles stood among the sticks of grease-paint. Sir Ernest Foster was replacing his wing collar with a semi-stiff one: the Vicar was dashing cold cream on Robin's face. Kershaw was greeted with a salvo of remarks. Among the private jokes and the ridiculous excitement Garner felt as awkward and supercilious as a man in the company of two lovers. Kershaw found a glass of warm beer for him and he sat sipping it, his bottom resting on the enormous black pipe of the central heating.

Eventually they were left alone. Kershaw, in a striped

shirt and the trousers of the battledress, rubbed the black off his eyebrows with a towel. He turned to Garner with a face immediately more commonplace. 'You're a novelist, aren't you, Mr Garner?'

Not *the* novelist, Garner noted. Garner pleaded guilty.

'We had Priestley in Askington the other week. They've just rebuilt the Theatre Royal, you know. I met him after the official lunch, as a matter of fact. Fine chap.'

Garner again admitted the charge. Kershaw drank some beer and wiped his lips. He said: 'I hope you don't mind me saying it, but I can't imagine how you came to be a friend of Willie Widgery's.'

'We were at school together,' said Garner to excuse himself.

'I mean Willie Widgery's just an ordinary chap. I don't suppose he's been out of Askington three times in the last ten years – except to Grange or Harrogate for his holidays.'

Garner engaged the gears. 'Then doesn't that', he said, 'make it all the more strange that he should have gone away now?'

Kershaw took up the towel again and looked back in the mirror. 'Yes,' he said. Garner felt that a curtain had suddenly been lowered between them. There was a silence during which Garner found his mind a blank and nothing better to do than to drain his beer to the very froth.

'You have been friendly with Willie Widgery ever since school?' asked Kershaw. He stood up and unbuckled his belt. Garner saw before him the bulky and inexplicable box file of Widgery's letters and the copies of his own. 'Yes,' he replied weakly.

Kershaw said: 'I seem to remember you coming to the mill a few years ago.'

'No,' said Garner. 'No, I've never been to the mill.'

Kershaw's removal of the khaki trousers seemed an expression of surprise. Garner added: 'I haven't seen Widgery for a long time. Our – friendship – was – carried on through correspondence.' He wanted to take back that sentence and reframe it, but too late.

'Oh,' said Kershaw.

Garner all at once realized that there was a point to Kershaw's questions. Kershaw was suspicious of him – or was it merely dislike? Was he for Kershaw tarred with the same Bohemian brush as the unpleasant Rogers? Garner for a moment wished that he could metamorphose himself into respectability, change the tweed suit for bird's-eye worsted, remove the beard. He remembered how he had stood on the pavement of Percy Street with Roderick Fox, feeling that the mask of his body and clothes did not properly represent him. He put his beer glass down with a thud and deliberately acted the part the coarseness of his appearance demanded.

He said: 'Miss Widgery thinks her brother has run away with this young man Rogers. Did you know that?'

'Run away?' echoed Kershaw.

'Widgery was stuck on him, it seems.'

Kershaw's lips moved a little but no sound came out of them. At last he found a response: 'You mean you think that Willie Widgery is a nancy?'

'Well, yes,' said Garner, puzzled, 'if you want to put it like that.'

'Rubbish!' said Kershaw.

Garner raised his eyebrows.

'Rubbish,' Kershaw repeated. 'And I've known him these ten years – day in, day out,' he added meaningly.

'*I* didn't say he had gone off with Rogers,' said Garner hastily.

'I don't care who said it,' Kershaw was truculent, combing his fluffy cigarette-tobacco-coloured hair. 'And I might tell you that Miss Widgery or no Miss Widgery I'm going to the police next week.' He gave Garner a searching look and seemed a little reassured by what he saw. 'At first, you know, she kept putting me off. Said he'd gone to London on private business and all that. In fact she's never come straight out with it – and no wonder if that's the cock-and-bull story she's got to tell. These spinsters of forty-five!'

Garner hesitated. 'You know, Mr Kershaw, someone like Widgery – in Widgery's position – wouldn't advertise his – his peculiarities. I needn't tell you that these things go on well-concealed in the best of families.'

Kershaw compressed his lips, pulled at his little snub nose, and shook his head.

'Then,' said Garner, 'why has he vanished?'

Kershaw stood up and put on a brown check, green over-check, sports jacket. 'Police,' he said, finally. 'Police next week. Have another beer.' He tilted the bottle. 'Yes, we're in a fine old mess at the mill, as you can imagine.'

Garner felt suddenly weary. Blast Widgery, he thought, and all his mysteries. He conjured up, with tender nostalgia, his high-ceilinged Bayswater room and his books. Then, as they stood side by side drinking, Kershaw turned his head and said: 'He's a fine chap, Willie Widgery.' And Garner felt a sense of failure, a sense that with more finesse, a better presence, he could have served Widgery adequately. But as had been proved so often he was not that ideal person of his imagination: he was only himself.

*   *   *

Garner closed *Our Mutual Friend*, saw that the time was 12.20, and switched out the bedside lamp. The hour of reading had not quite soothed his agitated nerves and so with practised cunning he decided not on an immediate attempt to sleep, but stayed calmly on his back and stared at the dim shape of the early Victorian wardrobe. The gleam of light on the dressing-table mirror was like a distant lake. He belched and tasted beer beneath the flavour of the ham sandwiches that had been waiting for them when they had got back from Askington.

In his memory the car journey unfolded itself again, the flat silver shapes of hedges and trees, the partially-lit gloom of more trees beyond, rearing up and gliding past as the headlights of Widgery's car (he must have decamped in Rogers') nosed out the curving road. He felt again, too, the awful absence of conversation after the five minutes it had taken him to report his interview with Kershaw. And then as they had passed the severe dark façade of the Bell Arms, Miss Widgery had said to him something like, 'Didn't Mr Kershaw say something about William's work at the mill?' Garner had passed over this in his unthorough way, masking his lack of comprehension and disinterest by making a fuss of his job of getting out of the car and opening the gates to the drive. But now, as he lay with his arms folded behind his head, Viola Widgery's remark seemed to have importance. For he realized quite clearly that somewhere in the day's events resided the real reason for Widgery's disappearance and that he himself had missed it. He saw that Widgery had probably gone off with Rogers: what he didn't understand was what he could do about the

48

situation that had ensued. After all, people aren't usually wrenched out of the tenor of their lives to play a negative part. And yet it was fixed that he should return to London on the twelve noon train tomorrow without anything, so far as he could see, having happened.

Not, he thought, that anything really happened in actual life. And with that thought came immediately another – the thought of his marriage. He remembered how easily he had said to Alastair Cuff: 'I've lived alone for years,' and how once the words would have stuck in his throat, never to be uttered. Yet the determinate event represented by his wife's leaving him had not at the time seemed an event to him at all, for the ruin of his life had been achieved by long and cumulative crumbling, and the final débâcle had simply been the tiny removal of one stone. So, too, the pain of his loss had been such a drawn-out crescendo and diminuendo that he could not imagine it as pain. And when he thought of Victoria, his wife, he thought of a character out of a book, someone with clear edges but without emotional tone.

However, he must put his thoughts on a pleasanter track. His novel. It had reached the rewarding stage when enough had been written to give it an impetus of its own, in addition to the impetus of the plot and his ambition. So many threads had been introduced that some of them led away from the drive of the cloth and had constantly to be caught and brought back into the main pattern . . . He felt sleepy. He brought his arms under the bedclothes and turned on his side. The shape of the bed was unfamiliar, but its stangeness seemed almost to stimulate him to sleep. He smoothed the pillow with his cheek and closed his eyes. After a few minutes he found a pulse throbbing in his temple and turned over on his other side. There the pulse was worse and so he turned back, placing his head halfway off the pillow to avoid giving the pulse a sounding-board. He realized with exasperation that he was wide awake – wide awake and with the same anticipation of insomnia he had had before he started reading. He sat up and smoothed the hair off his forehead. The darkness of the wardrobe looked like a wide door. Cocky little Kershaw would now be sleeping easily. Garner felt a deep jealousy of the normal. He sensed the quiet spreading outwards from the house, the quiet of dull humanity resting, renewing itself for another day. His toes curled ominously with anger.

When he lay down again he found the pillow surprisingly and delightfully cool. His legs took an easy position. The pulses had gone. It certainly seemed as though he might sleep. But after a few moments he discovered that his eyes were still open: he closed them. His thoughts travelled on the surface of consciousness and no effort of relaxation could make them dig deeper. He set himself one of his usual anti-insomnia problems, not too easy, not too hard. Living English poets through the alphabet. Auden. American, perhaps. Allott, then. Barker. C was a little more difficult. Church. Durrell. E escaped him at first. Every was rather too recondite to be fair, but he certainly recalled a poem in the *Criterion* once ... His thoughts drifted off.

But still they were not thoughts that led to sleep. In fact he would never sleep, he decided in a fit of temper, and sat up suddenly and switched on the bedside lamp. By *Our Mutual Friend* the face of his watch looked innocently up: the hands pointed to the ominous time of 1.35. His eyes not yet accustomed to the light, he started reading, but without full concentration, hearing the slight flapping of the curtain at the open window and, far off, a motor bicycle on the Askington road.

He read: 'I would recommend examination of the basin in the saucepan on the fire, and also of the potatoes by the application of a fork.' Of course, he thought, the point was that he was hungry, in spite of the ham sandwiches. The northern air was keen. He felt the saliva running under his tongue and looked round the bedroom as though he might see some food lying miraculously about. If he could only find a few biscuits or an apple, with a cigarette to follow, sleep would surely be assured. He rose and put on his dressing-gown and slippers.

In the dark, so as not to arouse Miss Widgery and the domestic, he found his way tortuously to the dining-room where, before proceeding to *The Years Between*, they had had high tea. He shut the door carefully and put on the light. Sure enough, on the sideboard was a biscuit barrel full of bath olivers. He took out three and then, greedily, two more. He stood with his mouth full, munching. Outside the window a tree moved against a dark grey sky dappled with darker clouds.

He prowled round the room. By the fireplace was a wicker rack which held some old copies of *The Times* and a *Good Housekeeping*: by the rack a table with an ashtray and some books – Trevelyan's *English Social History*, a novel by Mazo de la Roche, and a worn blue pamphlet, with the orange-red label of the London Library on its cover, called *Tennyson's 'Maud' Vindicated.* The magazine and the novel clearly belonged to Viola but the rest must be William's, and Garner was touched by this mute evidence of his life – evidence only of the ordinary, everyday part of his life, all the more pathetic for leaving out the strains and unhappiness, the ridiculous midnight weeping. Supposing the weeping to be true.

Garner carefully picked up a crumb or two and then crept back to bed with the remainder of his biscuits. He smoked his cigarette and read some more of *Our Mutual Friend*. Then he turned the light out. It was only half past two: there was the possibility of fully six hours of sleep. But not until four o'clock had gone and the first cautious twitter of birds had sounded in the garden did exhaustion wipe away some of the logic of his incessant thoughts and permit him to fall into a sound but brief slumber.

Chapter Four

GARNER, humming the big tune from the slow movement of Bruckner's Seventh Symphony, put on his black hat and opened the door of his flat. Immediately a small cat rushed in, uttering an indignant squeaking sound. This was the cat from the flat below. Garner made a leap to keep it from the uncleared table.

'Excessively ill-behaved cat,' he said, holding it in his arms, 'you must go out. I am off for my – um – inspirational constitutional.' The cat miaowed. 'Well,' said Garner, 'perhaps there is time for just a brief snack. Fortunately, I opened a tin of sardines for breakfast.' He gave the animal a sardine on the saucer of his breakfast cup of tea.

Garner watched it eat. 'You are an emaciated cat,' he said, licking the oil off his finger and thumb. 'Greedy and emaciated.' The cat cried for more but he took it out of the flat with him. It followed him downstairs, and he regarded it severely as it made as though to go with him into the square. But suddenly it sat down and began to wash. Garner walked off humming.

He was in a good mood. In his wallet was a cheque from his agents for £47, his percentage of the royalties on the Dutch translation of *Goats and Compasses*, and he had forgotten that the Dutch rights had ever been sold. His night's sleep had been satisfactory, despite waking early. Before breakfast he had finished typing a story that as well as its intrinsic merits bore all the hallmarks of being a cert for the rich American market. He might well include his bank in his stroll so as to pay in the cheque. Really, it would bring his account to such a figure that sufficient might be hived off to buy a parcel – a tiny parcel – of shares. Perhaps he would lavish threepence on the *Financial Times* to see the present price of the various securities that he watched from time to time for possible purchase with the detached but affectionate interest of an uncle towards his nephew. Though both must be considered, he might buy machine tools rather than armament equities. One must turn to some personal advantage the frightful times in which one lived. We disillusioned denizens of the thirties, thought Garner, are certainly the ones best fitted to play the stock markets of the forties.

He had turned out of the square away from the Bayswater Road and now wandered in the decayed streets towards Paddington. This neighbourhood and its seedy inhabitants had no power to depress him – on the contrary. It reminded him of the streets of Crewe which he had prowled as an adolescent and which had given him his roots in the world. He thought of his dead father, that improvident provincial journalist, and realized for the first time that his own provident character was the simplest kind of reaction from his father's, and a reversion to the type of his forebears, generations of respectable, scraping petty bourgeois.

Some women were already on their way to the shops, dragging or wheeling male children whose obstreperousness was, it seemed to Garner, a reflection only of the temperament of the fathers – so worn and cowed were the mothers. Already his thoughts were taking on that generalized tone which so stimulated him for the work which awaited him on his return. Soon the digestive rumblings of his subconscious would throw up the hint that would enable his novel to take the next leap forward. Then he would close his mind to the more detailed formulations of description and conversation and walk quickly home, knowing that at his desk six or seven hundred words would stretch their complicated tendrils, not easily but with a dogged persistence, across his paper.

The Bruckner tune emerged from his closed lips. It might be worth while to find out just why it was on his brain – as one sometimes deliberately traces back a train of thought. The melodies one wakes with: there was an image in that. He took a turning which would lead him eventually but not too suddenly to his flat.

He saw when he got back to the square (after he had been unable to resist taking in the bank) that in front of the house was a motor-car, a dashing black sports model. His heart sank: he imagined Roderick Fox or some other rich bore come to visit him, and his morning ruined. But when he got closer the man in the driving seat proved to be a policeman. The family in the lower flat, for so long a menace to his peace, had at last offended the peace of the larger community.

On the flight of stairs to the first floor he encountered two men on their way down. The elder, a person fortyish, who wore a brown trilby over a sallow face adorned with a thin moustache, spoke to him.

'Excuse me, sir. Are you Mr George Garner?'

'Yes, I am,' said Garner, and then realized that the two were policemen in plain clothes. In spite of his clear sense of the absurdity of the emotion his heart started beating as though he had been running with all his might. His guilt must surely show on his face – the guilt for which his thoughts tried rapidly to find a cause. Still more absurdly he remembered his speeches at anti-fascist meetings in the thirties. Since then his life had been innocent.

'Could we have a word with you, sir?' asked brown hat. 'We are police officers.'

'Certainly,' said Garner, 'certainly.' He led the way to his flat, despising himself for his excessive amiability, his secret desire to prove himself a citizen of whom these men could approve. When he had let them in the three of them stood strangely in the middle of the floor.

Brown hat said: 'I believe you know a Mr William Widgery.'

Garner's tension was relaxed. 'Won't you sit down?' He dragged out two chairs. 'Cigarette?' Both men took one from his case. 'Yes, I know Widgery, of course, except that I haven't seen him for a very long time. We've corresponded for a number of years – since we were schoolboys almost.' The two men smoked stolidly. Garner realized that he had been so concerned with his own emotions that he had not asked about Widgery. 'Have you found him then?' he asked.

'Found him, sir?'

'Yes,' said Garner. 'He was – er – missing from his home near Askington. I was there at the week-end. But you will know all this.'

'Yes, sir. He was reported as missing. Have you seen him in London?'

'No,' said Garner. He was trying in vain to see these men not as symbols but as earners of a weekly wage, with families, an interest in racing, ordinary feelings. He suddenly perceived that there was something unspoken behind their questions and became apprehensive again. 'Are you from Askington?'

'No, sir. X Division, Metropolitan Police. So you haven't seen Mr Widgery since he was missing?'

'No,' said Garner.

The elder policeman deposited some ash in the turn-up of his trousers. 'Mr Widgery was found in the Thames at Shadwell in the early hours of this morning.'

'Oh,' said Garner. 'Dead?'

'Yes, sir.'

Under the eyes of the two policemen Garner's reaction was so encased in self-consciousness that he did not know what it really was. He said, with an ease and aptness that pleased him, 'Poor Widgery.'

'We had been advised already of his disappearance by Askington. When we found him they got your name and address from his sister.'

'Was it', Garner was about to say suicide and then cunningly changed his mind, 'an accident?' Both men looked away and he saw that he had not been so very cunning. If suicide had not been in his mind he would not have put the question.

'I don't know, sir,' said brown hat.

'Poor Widgery,' said Garner again, but the formula seemed to have lost its efficacy. 'Well, thank you very much indeed for telling me about this.'

The elder policeman said: 'It seems that the sister is prostrated with shock and not available for the journey to identify the body. She suggested that you would be kind enough to do that, sir.'

'Of course,' said Garner. 'Any time.'

'We have a car outside.' The two men rose and Garner

looked up at them for a moment as though he were being kidnapped. 'It won't take very long,' added brown hat.

On the way downstairs and into the car Garner spoke volubly so that no one who saw them should imagine that he was being arrested. Sitting next to the elder policeman in the rear seat he fell silent and remembered how long it had been before they had told him that Widgery was dead. Was the delay sinister? Could they possibly think he had anything to do with Widgery's suicide? Or was it merely, as was most probable, an example of the automatic tactics of authority – to let the other man do the talking? Since he was not in the least involved in the affair, thought Garner, either emotionally or factually, all he had to do was to sit back and observe. It was, after all, excellent material for a novel of action that one day he might amuse himself by writing.

The mortuary, dingy yellow brick at the end of a cul-de-sac, gave him all the same a quiver of apprehension – the actual chair at the end of a nonchalantly anticipated dental appointment. But he told himself that by closing the channels from his senses to his mind he could stand any ghastliness. He duly closed the channels and followed the plain-clothes men. The mortuary keeper seemed to be expecting them. He led the way through an office to a large bare room whose significance Garner, his imagination running on stone slabs, did not at first grasp. The mortuary keeper went to the wall and opened one of a series of small doors lining it. And then, before Garner had realized what he was doing, he gave a strenuous pull and brought out through the door and into the middle of the room a trolley and a breath of chill air. On the trolley was a long shape covered with the kind of blue-and-white-striped material of which butchers' aprons are made.

Garner felt his arm grasped by the elder policeman and himself propelled towards the trolley with the gentle but inexorable power used by doctors or nurses to enable the eventually astonished patient to achieve almost under his own volition some therapeutic horror. He found that his legs were trembling.

The mortuary keeper folded back the butcher's apron. In the middle of the haze caused by his suddenly throbbing temples Garner saw the ivory face of William Widgery staring with wide blue eyes at the ceiling. The moustache and the curling hair on the chest were, to his surprise, iron-grey – grey but so vigorous-seeming that it was unbelievable that their owner was dead.

Garner nodded. 'Yes,' he said, and then intending to say something more found that he could not speak. The cloth was replaced. As he and the policemen turned away he heard the wheels of the trolley on the stone floor and then the iron slamming of the door.

In the office he found the elder policeman holding out a packet of cigarettes. Gratefully he took one and smoked in the luxury of accomplishment.

'You'll be wanted for the inquest, sir,' said brown hat. 'You'll get notice served on you.'

'I see,' said Garner. 'Thank you.'

The policemen gazed at him sympathetically. 'The police car will run you home,' said the elder.

'No,' said Garner. 'No. I'd rather walk.'

'All right, sir. Nothing like a bit of fresh air.'

'No,' said Garner, 'nothing like it.'

In the street he was disconcerted to find that he was in

fact breathing the air in great life-giving gulps. He walked briskly to put some distance between himself and the mortuary, to find again that comfortable communion with himself, that enjoyable succession of habits, that the police had interrupted. But still impressed on his vision was the unbelievable image of Widgery's dead face. For a moment Garner's eyes were blurred with tears: yes, he was moved – angry, even. He was angry that Widgery – his gentle, ironic correspondent – should have been inveigled into passion and then despair by that vague but certainly money-grabbing youth.

Garner recalled the previous Sunday morning in Askington. During his wakeful night he had thought of something he might usefully do about Widgery's disappearance – call at Rogers' digs to see if a forwarding address had been left. Over breakfast Miss Widgery had jumped at the suggestion and later telephoned Kershaw to find out where Rogers had lived in Askington. They had driven silently into town, Garner exhausted by his wretched night but, as usual after sleeplessness, his senses sharp and his mind furiously active. For the first time he had been aware of Viola Widgery as someone with whom he might make more than conventional contact, as he threw glances at her fine, pale profile. Perhaps she, too, had failed to sleep: and he imagined her in her room smoking the cigarettes of crisis, reading her novel, her feminine, selfless emotions probing the raw place of her brother's absence.

The car had been parked at the end of a street of small terrace houses looking on to a children's recreation ground, on to the grass worn bald, the crude iron swings and bars like medieval instruments of torture. Garner had gone along the street to the house, the dust of the manufacturing town blowing into his tired eyes. And as he rang the bell, noting the net curtains and a huge-bellied yellow vase containing a flowerless plant peeping between them, Rogers became suddenly real for him. He imagined the handsome young man in his room, lolling on a horsehair sofa, the packet of cigarettes, the quart bottle of beer, the Penguin greenback, incongruous modernities among the Edwardian artisan respectability.

The door had been opened by a fat woman of fifty in an overall, her hair reinforced with Kirby grips. Garner told his story. 'I'm a friend of Mr Rogers. I think he left Askington rather suddenly. Did he give you an address? I'd like to get in touch with him.' He had not left an address, said Rogers' landlady. Had she any idea where he had gone or whether he would return? 'I fancy he's gone back to Lundun,' she said amiably but without interest. Clearly Rogers had paid up his rent, and had carried on his private life otherwise than in his digs.

Garner had returned to the car and reported to Viola Widgery. A church bell had started to toll. There was an hour before Garner's train left and they looked at each other almost frightened at the boredom and unease that lay ahead of them. Miss Widgery had driven slowly to the station, refused Garner's repeated offers of release. The refreshment room on the platform was closed. They paced up and down, passing again and again the row of new motor-cycles, the smell of stale fish, the cardboard boxes labelled *We Are Live Chicks. Handle Us With Care* from which there came a slight squeaking and knocking and a glimpse of yellow fluff. Garner had made a mental note of the cardboard boxes, to be used later as a symbol of the pathetic human condition, or something. At last, like the curtain on an unbearably tedious play, the train had descended on them, and they parted indecisively, a score of questions unasked – unaskable. In the carriage Garner had unzipped his hold-all and pulled out *Our Mutual Friend* with the guilt and relief of one who has just left a mortally ill relation.

And now, he thought, all the tension was at an end: after a morsel more of unpleasantness he could wipe Viola Widgery from his conscience. He felt hungry and thirsty all of a sudden, and cast his eyes down the street for the Ionian white and gold of a Lyons. He visualized with pleasure the bath bun and coffee at a quiet table, and patted his side pocket to make sure he had his notebook, for a tea-shop invariably stimulated his reflective faculties. The morning might not yet be completely ruined. He looked at his watch, saw with surprise that it was already 12.40, and then, in a slight panic, remembered that he had a luncheon date. With luck he might yet avoid the expense of a taxi. He quickly worked out his route and hurried to a bus-stop.

Power House spread itself along the Embankment like a barracks, all windows and red brick, except for some perfunctory stone urns and caryatids at the entrances. Garner found the door labelled *Power Manufacturing Corporation Limited*, as he had been told, and went through it into a hall of marble veneering and glossy mahogany. At the top of a short flight of stairs was a commissionaire in his glass cubby-hole. 'I have an appointment with Mr Claude Perrott,' said Garner.

The commissionaire looked critically at Garner's hat, beard, and tweeds, put on some steel-rimmed spectacles, and consulted a book. 'What name is it?' Garner told him.

'Mr Garner. That's right, sir.' The commissionaire took a fresh look at Garner, keeping his finger at the name in the book as though the unlikely connexion between them might vanish if it were not kept under observation. Then he pressed a button and a pageboy appeared. 'Take this gentleman to Mr Perrott's secretary,' he ordered.

As the lift slid up six floors Garner removed his hat and surreptitiously arranged his hair with his fingers. He was thinking that he ought to have had a wash even at the cost of being still later. He scraped some dirt from one thumbnail with the middle fingernail of the other hand. He tentatively touched his forehead, found it greasy, and rubbed it with his handkerchief. Before he could investigate how satisfactory a smear of dirt he had achieved, the lift gates opened and the pageboy ushered him out and down a corridor to a mahogany door.

The door was opened in response to the boy's knock by a blonde young woman who smiled and said: 'Come in, Mr Garner.' She took him through another door into a small waiting-room panelled in fudge-coloured oak. She said: 'You know Mr Fox, of course.'

Fox was sitting in a tubular steel chair, reading the *New Yorker*, perfectly groomed.

'Yes,' mumbled Garner. 'Sorry I'm late, Roderick.'

'Hello, George,' said Fox.

Garner sat down and half-reached for a periodical from the table but then remembered his social duties. He looked at Fox, and Fox obliged by speaking. 'I didn't think we'd bring in Sir Theo at this stage, George.'

'No,' said Garner.

'In fact I haven't approached him yet. This is just a dummy run. Perrott wanted very much to meet you.'

'I want to meet *him*,' said Garner. 'The idea of him fascinates me more every time I think of it.'

Fox narrowed his eyes ambiguously. The young woman, who was Perrott's secretary, returned and led them out of the waiting-room to a long narrow office whose windows looked down on the river. At one end of this room was a walnut desk: at the other a matching table studded with chairs. The walls were painted grey and quite bare, except that over the electric fire inset in the longer wall there blazed a crimson and blue painting of flowers by Matthew Smith. Behind the desk stood a medium-sized, middle-aged man smoking a cigar.

'George,' said Fox, 'do you know Claude Perrott?' Of course I don't, thought Garner: this was always Fox's formula of introduction and it always irritated him. He shook hands. They all sat down. The secretary asked Garner and Fox what they would have to drink. Perrott had put his cigar back in his mouth. He said to Garner: 'I hope it hasn't proved inconvenient for you to come here.'

'Not at all,' said Garner, thinking that if this man was implying that he was late he would bloody well ignore the implication. He saw out of the corner of his eye that someone was setting the table for lunch. His sherry appeared on a small kidney-shaped table at his side, with a box of cigarettes bearing a Jermyn Street name. He took a gulp of sherry and further occupied himself by igniting a cigarette.

Perrott had an unwrinkled well-filled face the colour of a manilla envelope – the face of a man who eats plenty of proteins and can smoke cigars right up to mealtimes. The cigar he kept in his mouth, rolling it a little between his lips: it was going well. He wore a double-breasted flannel suit, of a grey so dark it was almost black, a white silk shirt, and a rich tie in tiny blue and white check – expensive and becoming clothing but not quite that of a gentleman.

'We can take it,' he was saying, 'that the logistics of this little venture are well and truly laid on.' Garner nodded needlessly, for Perrott went on immediately, 'I am quite ignorant of these things, Garner, but just what ought a literary periodical to say at this moment of time?'

'Well,' said Garner, choking a little over his sherry. 'Imagination. Before the war . . . there was . . .' He put down his glass and started again, feeling his ears getting hot. 'It's rather difficult to explain without going into a lot of history. You see the 1914 war brought home to artists the overwhelming necessity of taking events into account in their art – events on the social scale. But only while the war lasted. In the twenties there was a reaction again in favour of art for art's sake.' He was launched. 'Not a reaction to pre-1914. The experiments of the twenties, the break-up of forms and the evolution of new forms, was necessary and valuable – not reactionary at all, in fact. But there was something missing which the social concern of the thirties tried to correct. Where the artists of the thirties went wrong was in trying to cure the sickness of art and the world with remedies borrowed from politicians. Artists spent their time at meetings, in committee, reading economics – and made their art out of the surfaces of their lives, their physical, bread-and-butter concerns. And bread and butter includes fear of bombs and whips.'

'So *Light* as you see it, George,' said Fox, managing to put in his oar at last, 'will eschew politics.'

'It ought to take note of politics,' said Garner. 'Take note of everything which goes on now, at this fag-end time of the forties, of importance to people as a whole. The artist must never forget that he has to live like other people, in their world. But the resources of the artist are deeper and subtler than the resources of economists and politicians. And problems which are insoluble on the level of conferences, monetary exchange, treaties, strikes, atom bombs, concentration camps, can be resolved by the artist's imagination. Not only for the artist but for other people, too. It's a platform for imagination – to put the point at its simplest – that I would want to provide.'

Perrott laid his cigar, which was finally down to the butt, in an enormous ashtray made of a veined, greenish stone, like a fitting from a film-star's bathroom. 'That is what I would want to provide, too,' he said.

'And because of your generosity and vision, Perrott,' said Fox, 'we need compromise with no one. No need for middle-brow names to try to win a spurious market for it. And our editorial policy will ensure that it won't be used by any didactic clique.'

Garner squirmed: Fox was like his own image in a bad mirror – everything there but just slightly wrong, dim, ill-proportioned.

'Yes,' Garner said, 'English writing has been crippled for several years because it hasn't had an outlet for its native vein of high imagination. I'm sure that the simple existence of a serious medium will bring out new writers and new work from writers we perhaps considered exhausted by the war, the change in their way of life forced by the war.' He thought of himself. 'There are things in writers' minds, maybe even in their desk drawers gathering dust, which just lack the sympathy of an editor – an editorial board,' he added, looking at Fox and Perrott in turn, and becoming aware of a slight change in their attitudes, the atmosphere, which indicated that it was time for him to stop talking and to start lunch. He blushed a little and drained the topaz of sherry in the bottom of his glass.

Perrott rose. There was a discreet chink of china from the other end of the room. The great industrialist had obviously heard enough of art for the time being and was hungry. 'Extraordinarily interesting. Come along, gentlemen,' he said.

The meal was served by a man in a white jacket but Perrott's secretary hovered and saw to the wine. Garner occupied himself purposefully with the rich pâté, and then the lobster encased in a delicious cheesiness, the bread crusty but flaky, the abundant chilled butter, listening to Fox chattering, watching the secretary manoeuvring the long-necked bottle like an obscure symbol. She was a girl of some attractiveness, her natural plumpness fined down in her face by a diet, perhaps (thought Garner), and in her body by a severely-cut suit in a plain cloth just lighter than navy blue.

How could one get, if one wanted to, all this into a novel? The power behind the luxury, the figures and men and machines behind the power? Perrott's desk had been empty, even of a pen. Perhaps he never wrote: a file was merely opened and put before him, and he then nodded or shook his head. Somewhere in other rooms of the building ingenious men sat in front of books on company law, ledger sheets, reports on technical processes, with trade-union leaders, secretaries of trade associations, spoke on the telephone to members of parliament for industrial divisions, factories on bypasses and coalfields, stockbrokers, authors of economic classics, bankers – but for Perrott everything was rendered down to the naked bones of a question. Shall we do this? And the cigar made its indication.

'I can't take my eyes off your magnificent Matthew Smith,' Fox was saying.

Perrott had his back to the picture but he did not turn round. 'Yes,' he said, 'it is a good one, I'm told.'

Fox laughed his fox's laugh. 'Surely you don't need to be told. Haven't I heard that you are an authority?'

'Not an authority,' said Perrott. 'Nor a collector, even. A speculator. There is a rationale of picture buying just as there is of stock-and-share buying. In any market there always exists the possibility of profit. Some think that modern art has been fully discounted. True, the profits in the Impressionists and the Post-Impressionists have all been made; but there are painters of this century still neglected – established painters. Even Picasso, to take a rather comic example – it is obvious, when you think about it clearly, that the prices of Picassos in the fifties will be higher than they have been in the forties. Of course, you must have a fair amount of capital if you are going to invest in Picassos now. But the price – ex studio, not ex gallery – of the paintings of any promising painter of thirty-five, say, is sufficiently low as to compensate adequately for the risk of his dying before forty-five or not being in the top flights after all.'

Fox laughed again. 'I think you're pulling our legs a little.'

'Not in the least,' said Perrott. 'In fact I'll pass on a tip. Buy Vaughans. But you won't follow it – though if I'd said buy Glaxos you would have been through to your brokers from the nearest callbox after leaving here.'

Emboldened by the Geisenheimer Rothenberg (of which the secretary had produced a second bottle) Garner said to Perrott: 'I'd like to ask you as a matter of curiosity what inspired you to the idea of financing a literary magazine?'

Perrott looked Garner in the eye, with the habitual calmness of expression that might have been humorous but was not. 'I have a son at Cambridge who is a very literary young man,' he said. 'He aroused my sympathies.'

'Most interesting,' said Fox. 'Does he write?'

'I understand so,' said Perrott.

Garner bad-temperedly put his last cubic inch of Gruyère into his mouth, feeling that he was being toyed with, that the whole project of the magazine was nonsense, that the next thing would be a long impossible poem from Perrott junior for the first number. The secretary came up to his side. 'Will you have brandy or Drambuie with your coffee, Mr Garner?' she asked.

Perrott was lighting a cigar. He looked at Garner calculatingly through the haze and said: 'Since I knew that you were going to edit *Light*, Garner, I've been re-reading *Goats and Compasses*.'

Garner looked up, as absurdly pleased as when he saw somebody in the bus or tram reading him. Perrott talked flatteringly.

In the hall, on his way up to his flat, Garner met one of the children from the flat below. She was holding the cat awkwardly round its middle – the cat, Garner found by the size of his concern, in which he was beginning to take a possessory interest. 'For God's sake put the thing down,' he said to the child irritably.

'Eh?' said the little girl, automatically, but releasing it

69

all the same. Garner saw, revolted but fascinated, that her scalp under the silky hair was encrusted with a thick scab of scurf: her face was pale, with shadows under the eyes that were almost blue.

'What do you feed pussy on?' he asked.

'Taters,' she said, and ran out through the front door after it.

In his flat he flopped into his tattered green armchair: really, he thought, Perrott can hardly work at all in the afternoons if he lunches like that every day. With his eyes closed he began to relive the whole scene, trying to make his thoughts jump the parts where he had behaved inadequately or foolishly. When Perrott had dismissed them he had said: 'If you want anything, get in touch with Miss Freeman. She has forgotten more about our affairs here than I ever knew.' And Perrott had lightly smacked his secretary's bottom, not vulgarly but as though he were bestowing an accolade. Miss Freeman had shown them out through the anteroom, already beginning to be thronged with suitors carrying files, and smiled them goodbye. Yes, she was an attractive girl: perhaps he really ought to get in touch with her. He began to daydream ludicrously and rather lasciviously, until he sat up suddenly and reminded himself that so far the whole day had been wasted.

He went over, put the records of the Dvořák Cello Concerto on the spindle of his radio gramophone and pressed the switch: romantic music to arouse the creative faculty. Then he walked into the kitchen and splashed his face with water. By the time he got back the orchestra had reached the statement of the long melody of the second subject. He stood with his face buried in the towel and remembered, profoundly moved, what he had forgotten for hours – Widgery's death. The pale face and grey hair in the mortuary rose before him – so grey, and yet Widgery was only as old as he. He envisaged clearly his own death not far ahead, the lonely death in this room. He lifted his head and saw the bearded face strange in the mirror. The solo cello entered. He finished drying his face and took the opportunity of coughing a couple of dry sobs into the towel.

Chapter Five

THAT was Tuesday. The next morning he worked well,
lunched cheaply in his flat off a tin of Polish meat loaf, and
afterwards went into Cuffs. There he got hold of a typist
and dictated some letters to people he thought well of,
telling them of *Light* and sounding them for contributions.
The thing was beginning to take shape in his mind. He
would rouse this rather neglected figure, set that promising one on a new and more ambitious tack, surprise the
other old veteran by putting him among the avant-garde
where it would be seen he half belonged. And what significant omissions he would have! Every time he thought
about the magazine his ideas expanded: he had bought a
small red notebook to devote to them.

The typist was called Miss Stance, a dumpy woman
who wore her grey hair parted in the middle and arranged
in twin parabolas over her temples before it gathered itself
into a large bun. She was deeply respectful to him but not
timid; an admirable woman: he would annex her. He felt
the empire of *Light* expanding. When he had finished dic-
tating he got Foster, the house-organ man, on the internal
telephone to order letterheads and discuss the ritual of
advertisers, advertising, and distribution. If Foster proved
too busy to handle this end a business editor must be
found.

Miss Stance returned with a cup of tea for him. 'And I
thought you might like a chocolate biscuit, Mr Garner.'

'Delicious,' he said. 'How on earth do you come by such
rareties?'

Miss Stance smiled complacently and effaced herself. Garner settled down to some long-delayed work on *Action Stations: A Rear Admiral's Story*. Ten minutes later the telephone rang.

'Mr Garner,' said Miss Cherry's Earls Court voice. 'Mr Kershaw.'

The name was lodged vaguely but uncomfortably in his mind, like a shred of meat in one's back molars. 'Kershaw?' he repeated. 'All right, Miss Cherry, put him on.'

'He's heah,' said Miss Cherry, 'in the general office, and wants to see you.'

'Send him up then,' said Garner, remembering with uneasiness and astonishment as he spoke who Kershaw was. Perhaps Kershaw was in London on holiday and wanted an introduction to literary or dramatic life. But when the little man confronted him incongruously across the manuscripts and page proofs littering the table, Garner felt that some misdeed or omission from his past had caught up with him. The seriousness of the occasion was marked by Kershaw's dark-grey, chalk-striped suit, the folds of the wide trousers, falling gracefully on the black pointed shoes, the knees supporting a black homburg hat made of felt as unyielding as three-ply board.

When Kershaw had been given a cigarette, Garner said: 'How did you know to find me here?'

'Miss Widgery gave me both addresses.' Kershaw looked rather embarrassed: he was no longer the cocky Thespian of Askington Town Hall. Garner was awkward, too; expecting the making of some new demand on him. Even the Rear Admiral's manuscript on the desk before him seemed a refuge of culture and calm which was being rudely denied him.

'It's a terrible business,' said Kershaw, speaking the syllables of 'terrible' as though they were hyphenated in the style of *Chicks' Own*.

Widgery's death, of course, thought Garner, who once again had forgotten it. He nodded. 'Terrible,' he said.

'Miss Widgery told me to tell you that she'd had your letter and that it was a great comfort,' said Kershaw. Garner felt momentarily elevated, as by a favourable review. Kershaw went on: 'She thought I ought to come down here to see what I could do. That it wasn't fair that everything should fall on you. I've got a room at the Regent Palace.'

'But there's really nothing falling on me,' said Garner. 'As you know, I've identified the body. I've got to go to the inquest on Friday. But otherwise . . . Naturally, if there is anything I can do . . .'

'Well,' said Kershaw, 'unless the police make her she won't come down. She's certainly in no fit state. What a business! A thing like this happening to Willie Widgery. I can't believe it yet, really. Have they found this chap what's-his-name?'

'Rogers?' said Garner. 'Do they know about him? I haven't said anything.'

'Well, he drove poor Widgery to it. He oughtn't to get away scot-free.'

'It may just have been an accident,' said Garner, who by now had convinced himself that it was so. 'There are lots of places where you can easily fall into the Thames. Certainly the police may think it was an accident.'

'Do you?' asked Kershaw.

'My views aren't important. And I've no first-hand evidence I could give about Rogers.' Garner fiddled with his fountain-pen. 'But I thought you disbelieved in this relationship between him and Widgery.'

Instead of becoming aggressive, Kershaw looked sheepish. 'What else can you believe in?' He stubbed out his cigarette, watched it carefully while he added: 'This thing has got to have an explanation.' Kershaw was still doggedly stubbing. 'I'm going to be quite open with you, Mr Garner. *I* suggested to Miss Widgery that I came down here. You know I made no secret up in Askington all along that the police ought to be told. Well, there's still something to tell, isn't there?'

'About Rogers?'

'Yes, about Rogers – and – and all about Mr Widgery and his work at the mill.' Kershaw's voice trailed off, and he looked at Garner as though he expected a question. Then he said: 'To put the case in a nutshell, Mr Garner, I came down here to find the officer in charge of the investigation and tell him everything I know.' Kershaw rubbed his little turned-up nose defiantly.

'Well,' said Garner, 'if you feel like that no one can stop you.'

There was a silence during which Garner was surprised to see Kershaw's face turn a bright pink. Then the little man burst out: 'The devil of it is I think the police are watching *me!*'

Garner stared at him, thoughts crowding his brain. 'Watching *you?* Whatever for?'

'It's all a lot of balls, of course,' muttered Kershaw. 'I'm damned sure there was a plain-clothes 'tec on the train down. And tailing me here.'

'Here?' echoed Garner. 'Do you mean they think –?'

But Kershaw was not listening: having managed to get

the beginning of his story out, he was rushing on as though reassuring himself. 'You see,' he said, 'during the war we had all sorts of difficulties at the mill. We did well, you know, but we were short of workpeople, and there were long hours and the blackout and all that. I worked hard, damned hard. Willie Widgery made over some stock to me in 1943, said I shared the worry, ought to have some of the rewards. Made me a director – with him and Miss Widgery. He was still the boss, of course, but there it is – now he's gone the thing falls into my lap more or less.'

'I see,' said Garner, inadequately.

'So if somebody pushed him in the river that somebody could easily be me – or according to the way a policeman thinks.'

'Were you in London, then, when Widgery was drowned?' Garner felt baffled.

'Of course I wasn't,' said Kershaw. 'But they could think I drove him to it – or got someone to do it for me. When the police are on your track, lad, they take some shifting off.'

There was obviously much to say, but Garner did not know quite what it was. He put his fountain-pen in his pocket and asked: 'So what are your plans now?'

'I haven't got any,' said Kershaw. 'I'm going to stay for the inquest and then I've got to make some arrangements to get – to get the body back to Bell.'

Garner remembered the undertaker's shed next to the Bell Arms. 'Yes, I see,' he said. His first fears of Kershaw impinging on his precious time revived. 'I shall see you again on Friday, then,' he added, with that bold stroke cutting away the dangerous interim.

'Aye,' said Kershaw.

At this acquiescence in the essential separateness of their two lives, Garner brightened. 'You ought not to worry about things,' he said with an almost genuine heartiness. 'I'm sure we'll find at the inquest that there will be no evidence other than will point to misadventure. In which case why go to the police?' Kershaw grunted. 'Don't you think, too,' Garner went on, 'that you may be mistaken about the detective? After all, this thing has been so – so extraordinary, so tragic, that I think we've all been under rather more strain than we imagine.'

'Well,' said Kershaw, 'I suppose we shouldn't make more mystery out of it than there really is.'

'I entirely agree,' said Garner. He was watching intently for the psychological moment to rise – as a man watches for the opportunity to leave a meeting before its end. Just one more twist in a harmless direction to the conversation ...

'There are enough damn worries these days,' said Kershaw.

'Rather,' said Garner, laughing falsely to cover his next move. And as he got up, he said: 'Well, you are managing to keep the factory ticking over?'

With a little reluctance Kershaw rose as well. 'Just about,' he said, and brushed the ash out of the crown of his monolithic hat. Garner saw him to the door: they manoeuvred a little there, like boxers in a corner, but in the end the adieus were not too prolonged.

It was 5.15. He would, Garner thought, give Kershaw a quarter of an hour to remove himself from the district, and then go and have a drink, several drinks.

By the lavatories in Leicester Square he bought an *Evening Standard*. The neon signs of the cinemas gave the illusion of night, but through the gulf of Coventry Street the sky was still lightish. The roosting starlings filled the air with their high multitudinous quaver accompaniment, turning the cars and the concrete into the features of wildest nature. The seats in the square were fully occupied, by the usual outcasts of the locality and people who had made them the site of a rendezvous. The milkbars were filling up, the pavement outside the Corner House was thick, the buskers gathered in the side streets with their banjos and sheets of paper, waiting for the first queues.

Garner slipped his copy of *Edwin Drood* inside the paper, tucked them both under his arm, and watched for a gap in the traffic to cross over to the Automobile Association corner. At Piccadilly Circus he went down the subway and came up again on the north side of Regent Street. He passed the street vendor of sexy magazines and turned into the Café Royal. He hesitated between the upstairs bar and the ground floor, and decided against the former's intimacy. He found the ground floor almost deserted, chose one of the red plush couches, and put his hat, paper, and book on the marble-topped table. An old waiter shuffled up and he ordered a Guinness. He propped his paper against the water carafe and stared at the print but did not take it in. His mind was full of the ambiguity of what Kershaw had told him. Could it be possible that Kershaw was involved in the events leading to Widgery's death – involved in a way that Garner could not yet see?

The Guinness arrived and he took a deep draught of it. Really, he thought, he felt about this affair something of what he felt at the beginning of the war – caught up in, guilty about, events for which he had no responsibility and which with a little more care he might somehow have avoided. But time passed, and the events accumulated and spread, and the situation became irrevocable. And yet the thing must end soon: Widgery would have to be buried, the coroner's jury bring in some verdict. Then he could go back to his life – if one could separate groups of events like that from other events that happened to one, and disown them. To none of his correspondents was he relating this episode – for all it bristled with opportunities for epistolatory brilliance – not even to Carl Henderson, a young man who had been under him at the Ministry of Information and was now teaching English Literature to the indigenous population of Jamaica, far enough away, one might think, for any confidence. No, the whole thing contradicted, offended, hurt, some deeply-held conviction about the nature of life, his life: it was not bathetic, boring, painful, quietly enjoyable, absurd, or meaningless. What, in fact, it was he did not quite know.

He finished his drink and beckoned. 'Another Guinness?' asked the waiter, in his old man's, middle-European voice.

'Please,' said Garner. 'Is there anything worth eating tonight?'

The waiter shrugged his shoulders. 'The ushual things. There iss some game pie – not baad.'

'Game pie,' said Garner, dubiously.

'Pigeon, you know. But not baad.'

'I'll think about it.'

The second Guinness did not go down with quite the glow of the first, but the day's tiredness began to fade and he felt the relaxation and promise of evening. The place was filling up: a few were eating pre-theatre meals. He ordered a third Guinness, lit a cigarette, and spread out the paper. But instead of reading it he thought about the novel he was writing. Its hero was founded on the young Alexander Pope – a boy, a poet of great brilliance, tiny, humpbacked, ugly. The boy becomes friendly with two attractive sisters from a higher social drawer, whom he finds are the first people to ignore his deformities and recognize his talent. He is introduced by them into their civilized world. He falls in love with one of them but she marries a member of her own set, commonplace in the boy's eyes, and eventually he is made to realize that the sisters' – and their world's – valuation of him and his art is far lower than he had imagined; that they have, in fine, other values which he cannot share; and after some tragi-comic episodes he is dropped back into his former life.

Garner realized that this was not only the myth of artist and philistine, of the deceit of appearances, which he intended, but also an allegory of his own life. He was astonished that he had not seen it before, and wondered how much of himself the story was betraying. And at the same time he felt a tiny seed of discomfort that this novel – and, he realized, his others – omitted some element from which his experience normally sheered off. Widgery under the butcher's apron, for example. That did not fit into the present novel, as his life usually fitted into what he was writing so that in some mysterious way a plot and a set of characters could soak up experience undreamt of at the time they were conceived. He took out his notebook and wrote: 'A novel is only able to grow through the nourishment provided by the life of the novelist while he is writing it.' What nourishment could he give his Popean young poet: or, to put the thing another way, what nourishment could the young poet take? The seed of discomfort seemed pretty solidly embedded.

He looked round for the waiter. The cigarette smoke was quite thick: there was a continuous hum of gossip, like the machinery of a factory. A girl, sitting at a table along the wall, was watching him over a tall lager glass. Instantly he acted with elegance the part of a man looking for a waiter. When he glanced at her again the chewing-gum-coloured hat failed to disguise from him the fact that he knew her – that she was, he realized after a second's puzzlement, Perrott's secretary. He smiled: she smiled back.

By the time he got his drink he had made sure that she was alone. He caught her eye again, lifted his glass, and gestured interrogatively with it in her direction. She nodded. He picked up his hat, book, and newspaper, and, concentrating on holding the glass steady and also moving dashingly, walked over to her table. In the aisle he dropped the hat, tried to rescue it, and slopped his drink. He had to leave the hat, its black bulk rocking gently on the carpet. By the time he had deposited his other traps on her table a waiter had come up with the hat, which he presented to Garner with, it seemed, an ironical air.

Garner sat down by the secretary's side, the flush growing from his beard up to his eyes. Nevertheless, he said what he had planned to say: 'This is a happy coincidence.' He was always rather archaically courteous to women until he knew them thoroughly.

'Yes,' said the girl. She seemed quite pleased for him to be there. 'Do you often come in here?'

'Very rarely,' said Garner, as though questioned about his spiritual beliefs. 'Very rarely. You?'

'Haven't been in here for years.'

'Coincidence was the right word, then,' said Garner. 'Do have a drink.'

She said she would have a lager. Garner ordered it, with another Guinness. Again as he had planned he said: 'You do get away from big business then at a fairly reasonable hour?'

'Sometimes,' she said.

'I thought Mr Perrott a very impressive personality,' he said. He was finding her easy to get on with and his flush was dying down. A nice girl, he thought.

'Yes, he's a remarkable man,' she said.

'Even a hero to his secretary,' said Garner. 'You know, I could do with having your job for six months – to get a good peep behind the scenes at high finance and so on. No novelist since Balzac has properly understood what goes on in the world.' Really, he was compelled to think, he did talk nonsense to women who attracted him.

'I don't think you'd learn much,' she said. 'A secretary's job is always the same whoever she works for. Accurate typing, good filing, an orderly diary – she's so gummed up with these she doesn't really know what her boss is actually doing.'

'But one would know what precisely Power Manufacturing Corporation does?'

'Well,' she said, 'Mr Perrott isn't exactly Power Manufacturing.'

'Oh,' said Garner.

'It's rather complicated.'

'Then don't let's go into it,' said Garner lightly, sensing that he was making no headway. 'People often ask me all sorts of things about Cuffs – the publishers – thinking I work for them. Well, I do work for them, but only in the way that enables me to know scarcely anything of what goes on there, and certainly to take very little responsibility for what they do. Publishers are the classic type of capitalist – producing for an unpredictable market and extremely unpredictable themselves.' The Guinness was certainly making him voluble. But anyway, he thought, it was only natural that in these circumstances a man should parade and display himself from every angle, like a courting male bird.

He pinned her down by ordering another round of drinks and then went to the cloakroom. As he stood in his porcelain compartment he had a strong feeling of all this having happened before: and so, he reflected, it had – drinking with a girl, the successive visits to the lavatory, each one more elated and anticipatory than the last. It had happened even with his wife: especially with his wife. And when he returned to the restaurant room the sensation was poignantly familiar – the smoke, the chatter, the many alien faces absorbed in their particular worlds, and a corner of it waiting, even anxious, for his return.

As soon as he sat down he asked: 'Are you free for dinner?'

She hesitated a second and said: 'Why, yes. Thank you very much. That is, if you're asking me.'

She smiled. He said he was asking her. 'I think we won't eat here,' he said, remembering the game pie. 'Drink up and we'll go into Soho.'

When they emerged into Piccadilly Circus they found the streets wet after a shower, reflecting the lights. In the side streets they edged past parked cars beaded with wet and men taking tarpaulins off barrows of fruit arranged on bright artificial green vegetation.

'Let's try Vittoria's in Dean Street,' said Garner. 'Do you know it? At worst there's always beef escalope – horse, perhaps, but tasty and nourishing. I'm told we all suffer from lack of protein these days, so I constantly do my best to remedy my personal deficiency. Diseases once peculiar to the kraal and the equatorial forest have appeared in Europe since the war: the medical profession, trained to recognize gout and apoplexy, are confronted by sprue and beri-beri and are baffled.'

He took her elbow for an instant to steer her across Shaftesbury Avenue and found her taller than he had imagined. She had put on a gaberdine raincoat to match her hat: he noticed again that the tight belt made her look slimmer than she really was. He continued to be slightly embarrassed that he had forgotten her name: but perhaps Perrott had never mentioned it. Under the sodium lamps her lips looked as black as a heroine's of the silent screen; but luscious all the same.

In Vittoria's they had spaghetti and then the beef escalope, which proved inevitable. Garner was glad to see that the girl had a hearty appetite. He had them send out for a bottle of claret, and by the time they had reached the apple fritters he could imagine nothing more satisfying than to take her to the cinema and there perhaps hold her hand.

'Do you want some cheese?' he asked.

'No, nothing more,' she said. 'I've had about ten thousand calories too many already.'

Garner said: 'I think I shall have just a little cheese. They often have Danish blue.'

He had found out her name: it was Sarah Freeman. The 'Sarah' touched him: it revealed the difference in their ages. It had been an old-fashioned name in his day: his contemporaries had been called Joan and Marjorie. He ate his cheese and looked at her complacently. She was, she had told him in answer to his questions, a Bachelor of Science (Econ.) of London University. Her parents were dead, killed in Barnes in an early air raid. She lived in Chelsea. She liked the ballet, the novels of Graham Greene, the poetry of Cecil Day Lewis. She used a perfume called Arpège by Lanvin. For her last summer holiday she had been to Rapallo. It was all as he might have invented it for a novel, but the statue was breathing, warm, and not boring.

Over coffee he broached the question of the cinema: she seemed a little uncomfortable. 'I should have told you before,' she said. 'I really must go soon. I've promised faithfully to put in an appearance at a party.'

Garner felt like a child who had divined some delicious treat and been proved wrong in its divination. He took a great gulp of coffee and burnt his mouth.

'I suppose you wouldn't like to come, would you?' she said, doubtfully.

'A party? Whose?' Now he could afford to be rather bearish.

'Oh,' she said, 'a couple I don't think you would know. The Cartwrights – she paints, he works for the British Council.'

'No, I don't think I know them.' He sipped his coffee delicately. 'Fortunately. Where do they live?'

'Highgate.' She added quickly: 'We could get a tube.'

He was so pleased that he could quite clearly see his behaviour as ludicrous. 'All right,' he said, laughing. 'I'll condescend to come to your party. But let's fortify ourselves with some more coffee and a couple of brandies.'

As they finally emerged from Vittoria's she stumbled and fell against him. He took her unfamiliar shoulders and gently restored her centre of gravity.

'I'm drunk,' she said.

'Rubbish,' said Garner. 'You caught your heel in the grating.' The momentary grasp of her body aroused the calculating but warm interest felt by one who smells cooking a long time before dinner.

The Cartwrights' house was semi-detached and Victorian, halfway up the hill. Lights and a hum of talk denoted the party. Garner and Sarah Freeman found the front door open and the hall deserted: coats and hats had already overflowed on to the floor underneath the row of hooks.

The talk could now be heard clearly: it was punctuated frequently by laughter. Garner congratulated himself on the amount he had drunk. They hovered a little in the hall, and then a girl in a frock of thick black and white stripes, her hair done in a fringe and horse's tail, came up the basement stairs carrying a plate of Ryvita spread with paste.

'Hello,' said this girl. 'Have a thing.' She offered the plate.

Garner turned away: even drink could not stand up to this. Sarah said: 'Not just now, thank you. Ought we to go straight up?'

'Rather,' said the girl. 'I'll lead the way.'

The party was going on in a large sitting-room on the first floor. About thirty people stood and talked, holding glasses, cigarettes, potato crisps, and little sausages on cocktail sticks. Another girl with a fringe, this one wearing a crimson velvet dress, stood behind a table in a corner dispensing drinks. She espied Sarah and Garner and called out with the vivacity of youth: 'Beer or cup?' They chose cup. Sarah said: 'I'll see if I can find Minnie,' and disappeared among the bodies. Garner was left alone on the edge of the hubbub, gloomily swishing round two bits of apple in his glass. He examined exhaustively a lithograph by Paul Nash hanging on the striped wall, then put down his drink on the turntable of an acoustic gramophone with an enormous horn and picked up a book by James Thurber. In fiction, he thought again, one would not dare to lay a scene so uninspiredly typical.

Sarah returned with a thin woman with short straight hair, dressed in black, a filmy shawl round her shoulders. 'Minnie Cartwright,' she said, 'George Garner.'

'I hope you'll forgive me crashing your excellent party,' said Garner, deciding to play a part.

'Oh, Mr Garner, of course,' said Mrs Cartwright. 'Delighted to have you.' Her rearrangement of the shawl was like a nervous tic. She took his arm. 'I would so like you to meet Bill Birkett – if I can see him.' Garner found himself dragged from his safe anchorage, picked up his drink, and cast a suspicious glance at Sarah to see if she were enjoying his predicament. But her regard was quite serious; and he realized that her critical powers were still rudimentary.

'I expect you've read this novel Bill has published,' said Mrs Cartwright.

'Not yet, alas,' said Garner, still acting. But he was beginning to remember who Birkett was: a sort of proletarian short-story writer who had once edited a magazine called *Hammer* – or perhaps *Forge*.

Mrs Cartwright discovered Birkett at length talking to two other men under a shelf of cacti. Garner was introduced and his hostess fluttered away. Birkett was a self-confident little man wearing a bow tie and smoking a cigarette in a holder. It seemed that he was talking about his novel: its possible serialization in America, his chances of selling the film rights. He generously included Garner in his audience. Garner watched him evilly, and thought that in the world of letters there were as many social distinctions as in the world of *À La Recherche du Temps Perdu,* and that there was nothing so painful for one of the higher orders as to appear among the lower orders and his status not be recognized and respected. Garner tried to recall whether it was Birkett who had written that recent survey of fiction which had dealt with *Goats and Compasses* so cavalierly: on the whole he thought not – Birkett was really not sufficiently exalted to be asked to contribute an article of that kind to a literary weekly. Birkett was simply an ignoramus, a nonentity, a bore. Garner could hardly bring himself to stay within the circle of men for the space of time which politeness and his shyness demanded.

Birkett addressed him in his petty bourgeois, Kentish Cockney voice: 'Do you systematically try the American market, Garner?'

The cutting edge of Garner's reply was blunted by his mumble and by his immediately afterwards draining his glass: 'I leave such things to my agent.'

'Ah, agents,' said Birkett, with infinite comprehension. 'Really, one might as well decide to abandon agents completely. A plan of attack, good records, a regular time for correspondence – one can do an agent's job oneself in a negligible amount of one's time, and far more efficiently.

Agents don't really know anything, I find, don't even know one's work . . .'

Garner at last got away under cover of another mumble. Let Birkett – and anybody else – think him as dull and tongue-tied as they liked: the writer's worth resided in his writing, not his effect at parties. He stopped at the table in the corner and swallowed another glass of cup. What a fool he was, he thought, to take these people seriously, to care about their opinions. Henceforth he would be the aloof man, cynical and sardonic.

He spent a little time outside in the passage, wondering where the lavatory was. He tried one door but it proved to open only on a room full of toys and a strong smell of drying diapers. The Cartwrights had bred, then, he thought with disgust. At the end of the passage he encountered a middle-aged man with a drooping moustache, and made his inquiry.

'I've been downstairs,' said this person. 'First door. This bloody fruit cup runs straight through you, doesn't it?'

By nine o'clock the party had thinned a little but showed no signs of ending. Those who had had dinner or decided to eschew it began to settle down – on chairs, divans, the stairs – and a rum punch made its appearance, tepid but strong. Garner found himself with the moustached man he had met in the passage.

'What's the punch like?' asked the moustached man.

'Pretty fair,' replied Garner.

'I thought so,' sighed the moustached man, with regret. 'But I daren't touch it. I shouldn't really be drinking this.' He held up his glass of fruit cup, as a doctor examines a specimen of urine. 'You wouldn't think to look at me that I was an ulcer patient, would you?'

'No,' said Garner, glancing about surreptitiously for Sarah.

'Yes, I'm on one of my good cycles and so I'm tempted to indulge. I shall pay for it, of course. Curious thing, I get both gastrics and duodenals. Sometimes a gastric, sometimes a duodenal. I prefer duodenals – more stubborn but less painful. Luckily I don't perforate – must have tough stomach walls. There's no doubt that the peptic ulcer is the revenge of nature for civilization. Why should I get them? I'm optimistic, not too hard working, don't drink or smoke very much. I put them down simply to history. Wars on the outside, ulcers on the inside. Don't you agree?'

'No,' said Garner. He felt the necessity to be frank, to be brutal, to be his true self: certainly the rum punch had a substratum of rum. 'No, wars are caused by conscious acts, ulcers come from the subconscious. There is a conflict inside you that you haven't told me about or that you're ignorant of. Almost certainly a sexual conflict.'

The neck and jowls of the moustached man went a deep red. 'I say,' he said, 'that's really going too far.' He turned and marched angrily to the other end of the room. Garner laughed: he had a sudden vision of all the people at this party – all the people of the planet – with their secret illnesses; a species ostensibly flourishing but containing the fatal genes which would soon make it incapable of succeeding in the battle with its environment. Incapable, for instance, of being able to thrive on the food it had gone to such trouble to supply for itself.

He saw Sarah come in at the door, and went over to her.

'Did you ever come across so many wet people?' he said. The alcohol, he felt, had removed several layers of the convention which separated them.

'Oh dear,' she said, 'you obviously haven't had enough to drink.'

'Too much,' he said. 'I can put up with people when I'm sober.'

He gave her a cigarette and a light. She held his wrist steady as she pulled at the flame. The gesture pleased him.

'You've got the rum-punch shakes,' she said.

'Nonsense,' he said. 'It's you. You unnerve me.'

'You unnerve *me*,' she said. 'Or you did at the office, and earlier this evening.'

'Did I?' he said. 'Why?'

'I can only tell you this because of the drink. Your beard and hat and – and taciturnity, if there is such a word. Frightening.'

'How very surprising and gratifying!' said Garner. 'So I made an effect on you. It was quite uncalculated. I always wear a hat; and a beard for that matter. I suppose I don't normally talk much. But I'm not surprised or gratified that you've uncovered my disguise and found the silly usual face under the terrifying papier mâché.'

She said: 'I expect I should find you frightening again in the morning.'

'No,' he said. 'The spell's broken. People aren't frightening. Perhaps when you meet them at first there is a frisson of something, but you quickly see the familiar pattern. Life isn't frightening, either – as lived by humans – because they immediately make human what might be frightening. If I render myself clear.'

'Not very,' she said. 'Let's have some more punch.'

* * *

He found himself reclining on a divan, and struggled to a more or less sitting posture. Sarah had disappeared again. Perhaps he had been asleep. The party continued, anyway, though it must be late. A plump girl by his side whom he did not know said: 'Don't rock the boat, darling.' He conceived the idea of kissing this girl. She gave a complacent little scream. 'Help,' she cried. 'I'm being raped.'

A young man with a crew-cut on the other side of her said to Garner: 'Excuse me, sir. My bird, I think.'

'Sorry,' said Garner. 'I mistook her for my aunt.' He sank back on the cushions.

The man with the crew-cut was talking to a man with sidewhiskers. 'Believe me,' he said, 'there is something on the face of a man who has died a violent death that is absolutely unmistakable.'

'Can't say I've ever noticed it,' said the man with sidewhiskers. 'In the desert I wasn't in the habit of stopping to gaze at goners.'

'This is my point,' said the man with the crew-cut. 'The corpse that has been suddenly cut short has a living look – surprise, fear, and so on. With a natural death the look is quite inhuman.'

Garner sat up again. 'You are absolutely right – if you'll forgive me breaking into the conversation. Absolutely right.' Garner listened to his own words with a sense of astonishment: how on earth did he come to know anything about the subject?

The man with the crew-cut said: 'Thank you, sir. I can see that you are a man of keen perception. No doubt you have some recent experience which bears out the truth of what I've been saying.'

'Yes,' said Garner, and then stopped, remembering Widgery in the mortuary. Did accidental drowning count as a violent death? 'Or rather,' he went on, 'it depends on what you mean by "violent death".'

'Aha,' said the man with sidewhiskers, 'this is a logical positivist.' He had trouble with 'positivist.'

'Take drowning, for instance,' said Garner. 'A man slips on some canine nastiness and falls into the river. Violent death?'

'Oh yes,' said crew-cut. 'Allee samee man steps off pavement and gets knocked down by a truck. So your man was drowned?'

'Yes, drowned,' said Garner.

'Perhaps you can speak as to street accidents as well?'

'No,' said Garner. 'Just drowning.'

'Now our friend here', said crew-cut, indicating the man with sidewhiskers, 'writes detective stories and simply ignores the fundamentals. What the English detective story lacks is realism – realism about death.'

'Realism about everything,' said Garner.

'No,' said crew-cut. 'Too much realism and it would cease to be the detective story. For one thing, motive. Why are people murdered?'

'Money,' said Garner.

'They talk too much at parties,' said sidewhiskers.

'They get murdered', said crew-cut, 'as a result of the operation of the forces of society. Murder is life carried on by other means. Do you agree?'

'I don't know,' said Garner.

'Just think of some examples,' persisted crew-cut.

'I don't have any examples,' said Garner. He felt the

93

room sinking away from his eyes again and had a keen desire to relapse on the cushions.

'Well, who pushed your drowned man in?'

'He wasn't pushed,' said Garner. 'He fell.'

'Social forces my fanny,' said sidewhiskers.

'Has all the punch gone?' asked Garner.

'That's the first practical thing that's been said for half an hour,' remarked sidewhiskers. 'I'll go and see. Wait till I come back before you murder each other.'

Just five minutes' shut-eye, thought Garner, and then he would find Sarah what's-her-name. He discovered that his head was lying against the plump girl's thigh. The knob of her suspender pressed uncomfortably into his scalp. He shifted his head a little higher and from this more advantageous position felt that he could listen quite interestedly to whatever the man with the crew-cut might have to say. He sensed that sidewhiskers had returned with some glasses, and heard him say: 'Good Lord, beaver's passed out again.'

Garner chuckled to himself and decided to open his eyes and wink at sidewhiskers to show him how wrong he was. And then he thought that he didn't care whether sidewhiskers was wrong or not, and so kept his eyes shut.

Some time later Garner looked up and saw that he was at Archway Station. With a brilliant ratiocinative effort he visualized the whole underground system: 'Tottenham Court Road?' he said, with what seemed to him extreme lucidity, to a man wearing a peaked cap who at that moment fortunately crossed his path. 'Last train's gone, mate,' said this man, and passed out of Garner's vision. Taxi, thought Garner, taxi, and damn the expense: he owed it to himself to have his weary body borne in comfort to Bayswater.

Under the glare the long road stretched away gleaming and deserted. Garner staggered across it. 'Pick up an all-night trolley bus, then,' he muttered. How had he got himself into this pickle? Vaguely he remembered coming downstairs with a man with a crew-cut, talking, insisting on finding his hat, talking, asking ineffectually for Sarah. And then everyone had bloody well left him. He stumbled over the kerb and kicked it viciously. 'If necessary,' he said aloud, 'I'll bloody well walk home.'

Chapter Six

EARLY in the morning he awoke and found himself in his own bed. He felt terrible but suddenly without the capacity for sleep. He tried to understand why his mood was one of overwhelming regret for lost opportunity, for something missed that was poignantly desirable. He squirmed in the bed and switched on the light to make the mood more easily borne. He saw the chair empty and his clothes scattered on the floor, and remembered the girl.

It was absurd to feel like this about her. He scarcely knew her. But the reason for his disquiet was clear when he analysed the situation. There was a biological attraction – the surprisingly slim waist, perhaps, or the surprisingly straight nose – and there was her desertion of him at the party. An adolescent situation which had simply revived the emotions of adolescence.

Garner got out of bed, contemplated his feet as though they were symbols which could lend purpose to everything, and then opened the curtains on an electric moon shining in the ambiguous blue of pre-dawn. He closed the curtains and went off to look for aspirins. Perhaps later in the morning he would ring her up at Power House. Or perhaps not. He could go at night again to the Café Royal. Absurd, absurd! He swallowed his aspirins and put the kettle on. He had an awful hour to wait for the morning papers and his post, for the day really to begin. He sat at the table, held his head in his hands, and groaned with boredom and self-pity.

Over the tea he read *Edwin Drood:* his faculties stirred

and he even made a note or two on the blank sheet at the end of the volume. All his books were thus annotated; neatly, with the appropriate page reference, against the possible demands of a review or essay. Today he would only read and make the leisurely reflective notes of an invalid. He would treat himself as a sick man, which he was. He would prepare coffee for breakfast, and eat the egg he had got on the ration earlier in the week. Perhaps it would soft boil . . .

When the newspapers arrived he dropped the egg into the pan of water he had ready simmering. Breakfast was not breakfast without the morning papers. He returned to the table and separated the *News Chronicle* from *The Times*, propping the former up against a tin of South African melon and lemon jam with pleasant anticipation. The aspirins had certainly worked wonders: it could not be said that he felt a sense of well-being but his head was no longer in loose pieces. He could not forbear a glance, while he waited, at some of the lesser items on the front page of the *News Chronicle*. A warning by the Chancellor in a speech at Wigan against the dangers of inflation almost pleased him as he thought of his provident little cushion of first-class industrial ordinary shares. And then a name leapt out at him from the print of the page, and he picked up the paper and held it in his clenched hands as though it might escape from him. There was a headline and about an inch and a half of story.

KILLED BY LORRY

Yesterday afternoon, in Piazza Street, Covent Garden, a man was knocked down and instantly killed by a lorry which mounted the pavement and afterwards failed to stop. A witness of the accident said later that the lorry appeared to skid. It was growing dark and

*there was no other traffic about. The police are appealing to any
other witnesses of the incident to come forward. The dead man is
believed to be Frank Kershaw, aged about 40, whose home is in
Askington, Lancashire.*

'Yesterday afternoon.' For a moment Garner thought
absurdly that it had been Kershaw's ghost he had seen at
Cuffs, and then realized that the man had been killed almost as soon as he had left him. Suicide? But the lorry had
'mounted the pavement'.

Garner put the newspaper down in such a way that the
item about Kershaw was hidden from sight. He looked
round the room to find some familiar thing to hook his
thoughts to so that they might continue in a normal and
undisturbing way. He heard the children from the flat below coming up the area steps with the abandon of the
drunk or mad, as they always did. Their cries faded into
the distance.

Garner's door bell rang. He started violently, as though
he had been caught in a disgraceful situation. He went to
the door saying to himself that his nerves were in bad
shape, that he ought not to drink, his calm manner concealing a hammering pulse. When he opened the door on a
telegraph boy he almost smiled with relief. But what had
he expected to find there?

He tore the rough, orange envelope with fingers that
trembled visibly, embarrassed that the boy should see the
betrayal of an emotion that – Garner told himself – he did
not feel. He read the telegram hurriedly and said: 'No
reply, thank you.' As he closed the door he thought that of
course there was a reply and that he would have to phone
'Telegrams' or go out to the post office. He read the tele-

gram again, trying to reconcile himself to the boring and inconvenient consequence of its contents.

REGRET TO SAY MR KERSHAW KILLED IN ACCI-
DENT LONDON STOP WOULD DEEPLY APPRECIATE
OPPORTUNITY OF TALK WITH YOU HERE IF AR-
RANGEMENTS PERMIT STOP KINDEST REGARDS –
WIDGERY

And then he conceived a cunning plan. Today was Thursday: tomorrow at three was the inquest on Widgery. He would go to Askington this morning, perform his melancholy duty, and be forced regretfully by circumstances to return early on Friday morning. And then the whole affair could be written off, forgotten – or incorporated into art. He combed his beard with his fingers, visualizing his journey to Euston, sitting in the train, the bus to Bell, greeting Miss Widgery – by a sort of sympathetic magic taking the effort and pain out of the unknown future. As he stood there he heard an incomprehensible little knocking from the kitchen. He went hurriedly to investigate it, and found his forgotten egg dancing about in the pan of boiling water. He turned out the gas: the thing had been cooking for at least fifteen minutes. But with the satisfactory emotion of successful salvage and notable economy, he realized that it would do perfectly to eat on the train. He lifted it out of the water and looked for a paper bag.

Once again he stood on the steps of Brick House; dirty from the train, gripping his canvas hold-all, apprehensive as before. Only this time his apprehension somehow involved himself. He did not quite see how he could continue to try for that detachment on which, like a sofa, he had rested during his previous visit when things grew too arduous. He pulled the bell as though it were some fatal lever. Rain dripped from the rhododendron leaves.

The maid brought with her an air as tragic as was consonant with her black satin and strabismus. He was shown into the sitting-room and Viola Widgery rose to greet him. They shook hands, and then, when the maid had closed the door behind her, something shifted slightly behind Miss Widgery's pale, composed features – the shifting of a fault deep beneath some smooth rock face – and tears gushed from her eyes.

Garner was amazed. Did she think so much of Kershaw? And then he understood that it was her brother she was weeping for, whose death had still to be incorporated into the relationship between them.

'I'm sorry,' she said, in a choked voice, as though she knew that for Garner feeling must be kept secret. 'It was just seeing you, knowing that you . . .'

But Garner, in spite of himself, was moved too, and stepped forward and took her upper arm and pressed it, as though it were a man to whom he had to communicate his sympathy. Immediately his tension lessened, and he felt a sense of what was almost happiness to know that he could enter, if he wished, into commonplace feelings and relations. He remembered how before his first visit he had visualized patting her shoulder reassuringly and how wide of the mark that visualization had proved to be. But now he had found the right gesture, found it without strain and almost spontaneously. As he held his pressure of her arm for what seemed long seconds, he saw out of the corner of his eye the delicate ivory lobe of her ear emerging from her cigarette ash-grey hair, and smelt a faint perfume.

They moved apart. What could he say? He nearly remarked: 'I managed to catch the 9.47.' But again he was taken out of himself by that strange sense of participating unselfconsciously in pathetically ordinary life, and said instead what seemed to him as soon as it was out monstrously foolish and sentimental: 'He looked wonderfully peaceful.'

'It sounds very conventional,' she said stumblingly, without looking at him, 'but I really don't know how I could have got through this time without feeling that I could rely – that I could count on . . .' She left the sentence unfinished and went swiftly out of the room.

Garner walked to the fireplace with the luxurious freedom of solitude. And yet he looked forward to Viola's return without any discomfort, feeling the long journey that bound him to his own existence dissolve, feeling curiously at home, ready to pick up a book or to eat or to discuss some domestic triviality which nevertheless had to be settled before life could go on. He realized with a slight shock that this was the atmosphere of settled married life which he had not experienced for years and which until this moment he had completely forgotten.

The windscreen wipers made two clear geometrical figures among the anarchic raindrops. Garner was not quite sure why they were going to what Viola called – as Widgery had – 'the mill'. They had not yet had the 'talk' that was the ostensible reason for his visit: they had left Brick House even before the tea-tray had put in its appearance. But when Viola had returned to the sitting-room there had been time for her to tell him what was still sending ripples of astonishment through his mind – that Widgery had appointed him executor of his will, jointly with herself. He must have looked his amazement because Viola had immediately said to him: 'It was a recent will. I expect William would have discussed the appointment with you if – if there had been time. I know that he intended to visit London to see you – just before Mr Rogers came up here. And then, of course, he seemed quite unable to get away.'

Except at the end, thought Garner.

Viola said: 'I do hope you'll accept the office, though it will be a trouble for you.'

'Of course I'll accept,' said Garner.

'I thought, if you agreed, that I would instruct our solicitors here to act for us.'

Garner nodded rather helplessly, feeling very unexecutorlike.

'They will be writing to you, naturally,' Viola continued, still regarding him. She said: 'You see how William thought of you.'

'Yes, I do.'

'He spoke of you to everyone, you know. I don't think he would have chosen anyone but you to turn to for – advice and so on.'

'I'm very touched,' said Garner, meaning it. 'I'd done so little . . .'

And then they had set off for the mill. It seemed that it was still going: there was a works foreman of phenomenal long service and Widgery's efficient secretary. And there was another firm – not precisely a rival, but in the same line of country – which had held out a helping hand, with an eye, no doubt, to the main chance of a controlling interest in the near future.

'What *do* you make at the mill?' asked Garner, feeling that he ought to know, that Widgery must obviously have mentioned it, but without the slightest idea.

'Radio components,' said Viola Widgery.

They had driven through Askington, its stone black under the rain, and now climbed up a long cobbled hill, rows of terrace houses punctuated by pubs and factories on either side. Miss Widgery stopped the car in front of a small flat-fronted building with a wide gateway at the side. By the door of the building was a worn brass plate with the legend 'Widgery Bros. Ltd'.

'Of course,' said Miss Widgery as they got out, 'we didn't always manufacture radio components. William started that in 1931, during the slump, and it gradually ousted the other things.'

'Widgery *Brothers?*' said Garner.

'My father and uncle,' said Miss Widgery. 'They are both dead now.'

The front entrance led into a narrow passage in which there was a frosted window marked 'Inquiries', and a door at the side which opened into a small general office where a boy was hastily concealing a copy of the *Wizard*. They went through this office to a room beyond. There Garner was introduced to Widgery's secretary, Mrs Dickinson, a diminutive woman with a Pekinese nose, protuberant eyes, and sandy hair. She had been expecting their arrival: a kettle was boiling on a gas ring next to the gas fire, and a tray was spread with buttered teacakes and cakes.

'How nice of you to have got tea, Bella,' said Miss Widgery.

Mrs Dickinson blushed. 'Oh, it's nothing much,' she said, and busied herself with the teapot.

'I bet you made the maids of honour,' said Miss Widgery. Mrs Dickinson shamefully acknowledged the fact. Miss Widgery said: 'I simply don't know how you find the time.'

Garner sat rather helplessly on an old horsehair chair, his knees crossed, picking fluff out of the turn-up of his trouser leg. Through the window, beyond a yard where the rain was bouncing in puddles, was the two-storey factory building. As Garner watched, a man in overalls came to the entrance to the building, looked out, spat into the yard, and went in again.

Mrs Dickinson offered Garner a piece of teacake. '*This* isn't home-made, you know,' she said bluntly.

'It looks very good,' said Garner. He took a bite and caught Mrs Dickinson watching his beard. She blushed again and retreated behind her typewriter. Garner wondered whether it would be too trite for him to comment adversely on the weather.

But Miss Widgery said: 'Now, Bella, I wonder if you've had the chance of looking through the files.' She turned to Garner. 'I telephoned Mrs Dickinson first thing this morning and asked her to go through the cabinets in William's and Mr Kershaw's rooms.'

'I've had a peep at all of them, Miss Widgery,' said Mrs Dickinson. 'They're quite in order so far as I can see. Of course I know every one of them, really, because I've been doing Mr Kershaw's work as well ever since that Miss Bloodworth left to marry her Pole. No, there's nothing in the mill that isn't quite usual so far as I can see.'

Garner looked at Miss Widgery, beginning to understand. Mrs Dickinson fortified herself with a sip of tea, and then battled through her embarrassment with a speech she had obviously long decided to make: 'I don't think you ought to worry about the mill, Miss Widgery. I'm sure there's nothing *to* worry about. I look at it this road. There was Mr Widgery's accident: that was the terrible thing. And then poor Mr Kershaw had to go to London, in all that traffic he wasn't used to – what happened to him there followed on, you might say. It does sometimes happen that way. You remember my cousin Bernard killed in the belting at Lees' just before Christmas, and his wife going ten days later. She took a chill at the funeral.'

Mrs Dickinson rose and walked briskly across for Garner's cup. Miss Widgery said: 'Perhaps you're right, Bella.' She was very pale.

'I'm sure I'm right, Miss Widgery,' said Mrs Dickinson. 'Now do try one of my maids of honour. Mr Garner too.'

After tea Garner and Miss Widgery went across the yard, through the rattle of the machine-room of the factory up to a small room which Widgery had rigged up as a laboratory. Mr Kay, the works foreman, went with them.

'I wanted you to see this place,' said Viola Widgery. 'It meant a lot to William.'

It meant nothing to Garner: he stared at the rack of test-tubes and played with a switch on a little electric furnace. 'It all looks quite complicated,' he said inadequately.

'He were a clever chap were Mr Widgery,' said Mr Kay, and then blew his red pitted nose and afterwards adjusted the waxed points of his moustache.

'Did anyone help him in here, Fred?' asked Miss Widgery.

'No,' said Mr Kay. 'Young David Knowles – Arthur's lad – used to come and clear up once or twice a week, that's all. But young David'll know nowt about it. Of course Mr Kershaw was in sometimes.'

They went down some roughly railed steps and into a large workshop where a number of motherly-looking women sat at benches doing something with wire. From two loudspeakers came a roaring reproduction of an orchestra playing 'Old Man River'. The women regarded Garner with interest. He shouted in Miss Widgery's ear: 'They all look as though they're sitting at home peeling potatoes.'

The party at length came again to the yard entrance of the factory. Mr Kay accepted Garner's offer of a cigarette, but no one had anything to say. The noise of the rain drowned the faint noises of the factory behind them. Mr Kay took the cigarette out of his mouth, tapped the ash off, and said: 'Well, there'll no one take Mr Widgery's place. There won't that.'

'No, Fred,' said Miss Widgery. She turned to Garner: 'I think we'll be getting along if you're ready.'

'Yes, I'm ready,' said Garner. What did it all mean, he was thinking: not only Widgery's death but the extraordinary activities of people in an industrial civilization; the loudspeaker music, the coils of metal shavings he had seen, like the hair of some fabulous redhead, the unbearable, but borne, din of machines; the *ad hoc* ramshackle factory, the filthy town; and his own little functioning brain with its alien, inhuman shape? How to lead up to points like this in a novel was the problem; the transcendental pattern made by three people standing awkwardly watching the rain, each with his own thoughts, brought together casually but surely with some arranged purpose: to describe the thing completely in its own terms – and to imply its meaning or lack of meaning in the terms of something completely irrelevant and uncomprehended: to select that ordinary feature of the outward which was the terrifying symbol of the inward.

Mrs Dickinson stood at the office door to see them off. 'They are nice people,' said Garner, opening the car window an inch to throw away his cigarette end. To his surprise he found that he was almost sincere.

'Yes,' said Miss Widgery. She changed into top. 'I'm glad you were able to come.'

'So am I,' said Garner. 'I see now more clearly how difficult it is to find any reason for – for things.'

'Do you think there is a reason?'

'I meant how senseless those two deaths were.'

She was not to be put off. 'But is there really a sensible reason?'

'I don't know,' said Garner. Then he came out apologetically with what he had thought when they were with Mrs Dickinson. 'Perhaps one ought to see the accountants.'

'I have,' said Viola Widgery. 'Before Mr Kershaw was killed. There was nothing wrong financially.'

He watched the windscreen wipers describe a few arcs and then said: 'You've done wonderfully in all this.'

'Oh,' she said, and her hands made a little gesture of disclaimer without leaving the wheel.

He felt once again the sense of relaxation in her presence. 'It sounds melodramatic and far-fetched,' he said, 'but what about the firm that's taking a friendly interest in the mill now?'

'You mean they wanted to take us over so badly?' She smiled. 'That's quite impossible.'

'So I imagined,' said Garner. 'You know, I'm sure Mrs Dickinson was right. Coincidence – she put it very well. It plays a bigger part in life than we're ever willing to admit. Novelists know that – even if they're too timorous these days to use it.' He was tempted to go on and talk about *Edwin Drood* but felt the occasion inauspicious. It was odd that he could say with ease to her things it would never occur to him to say to people he was usually with. If one were writing fiction for her eyes alone, now, how effortlessly the stuff would flow out. Perhaps she was his true level: ignorant enough to think him cleverer than he was, but clever enough to value what talent he had.

They went along in silence for a while, and then she said: 'It's the maid's half-day. I thought we'd drive back through Orton – it's not very far out of our way, and there's a public-house which puts on quite a good high tea. If you don't think high tea too barbarous a custom.'

Garner said that that sounded fine. They drove out of the north side of Askington. The tramlines came to an end and the road ran under a low railway embankment and then over a canal. A sparse wood fringed the horizon and above it the rain clouds were lifting away from a narrow band of livid sky. Beyond a church and a few houses was the pub, a stone box with a car park at the side.

They were a little early, they were told, for the high tea, and Garner suggested a walk. They went out at the back of the pub, through a vegetable garden, down a field path and into the low trees of the wood. The rain had stopped. A wind blew, rattling the ivy against the trunks of trees, and Garner pulled his great hat over his eyes, recounting to himself what he could remember of the dreadful party the previous night. Was it deliberately, or merely through the vicissitudes induced by the rum punch, that the girl had deserted him? He wondered once again how she thought of him in the realistic light of day: with boredom or indifference? Certainly not with regret, as he of her. He saw for an instant that frightful discrepancy between one's own valuation of oneself and other people's, and then quickly steered his thoughts away from it.

When Viola Widgery spoke he glanced up almost startled to find himself where he was. 'Looking through William's papers,' she said, 'I came across his file of your letters. I wondered if you would like it.'

Garner hesitated and coloured. 'Thank you. Yes, I think I would. Yes, indeed.'

'Did you ever regret – your side of the correspondence?' she asked, awkwardly.

'No, of course not,' said Garner.

'William was immensely proud of your letters, though I don't suppose he ever said so in his. Such things only come out when it's too late.'

Garner was moved, as though a critic had unexpectedly singled out for praise a quality of hidden and utterly private merit. 'I'm glad,' he mumbled. And then he added: 'I'd be very happy for you to keep the file, if you would like to.' He coughed. 'As a matter of fact I have copies of my letters. Always make a practice of it.' And as he looked at her quickly with a sidelong glance to observe how she had taken his confession, seeing her Burberry and black hat, the strong face with its bones near the surface, it came to him that he must start a file for his letters to her, for she more than adequately filled the gap caused by Widgery's death. He anticipated with a sense of pleasure the stream of words on which their future relationship would be borne.

When they got back to the pub the bar was open and Garner suggested that they cut the tea element out of their high tea and had a drink first. In the saloon a fire was blazing and a red-faced man of the commercial kind was drinking scotch and reading the local evening paper. Garner regarded the amber two inches in the glass and felt a sudden appetite for it. He brought a couple of doubles to the table in the corner where Viola was sitting. While they drank them she told him about the visit to Brick House of an Askington police inspector the previous evening. That was when she had learnt of Kershaw's death.

She said: 'And that was when I panicked and sent that telegram to you.' She swallowed some of her whisky. 'It seemed then – it even seemed so earlier today – that something, someone, was actively against us. I couldn't see those – those two calamities in any other way. But while we were at the mill I got things into their proper perspective.' She smiled. 'You are a very calming person.'

It was too embarrassing – and yet extremely pleasing. 'Am I?' said Garner. He felt a ridiculous urge to talk about himself. 'I'm far from inwardly calm. It's just that I don't show, perhaps, the quaking bog beneath the featureless exterior.' Why shouldn't he talk about himself for a change? Normally he never had the chance. 'But I certainly judge everything in the light of common sense – which few people do, even those who think they have common sense. And why I can do that is because I am emotionally obstipated. I feel things, but the feeling doesn't come out. Except when I'm writing.'

'No,' said Viola, 'you are not like your books.'

Garner was delighted with the remark: he experienced a delicious surge of optimism and happiness. Anxious for it not to fade, he said: 'Drink up and we'll have the same again.'

To wash down their fried plaice and chips, and apple pie, Garner ordered a bottle of South African hock. He said that he had a low blood pressure and wasn't really like other people until he had had two drinks – and then wondered if he had made the same remark to Sarah Freeman the previous evening. He drank most of the hock but insisted that Viola had a cherry brandy with the coffee that the fat, homely waitress produced reluctantly in substitution for a pot of tea. His faculties quickened. He observed with a self-conscious novelist's eye the elderly men in navy-blue suits, speaking with strong Lancashire accents, who sat at the next table, chaffing each other, talking about eccentric common acquaintances, enjoying their food – managers of small factories, he imagined. And he observed, too, Viola, seeing her for the first time as an equal, someone not much older than himself; the hands, not plump, but well covered, with creamy skin; the eyelashes curiously black against the light-blue irises.

Driving back to Brick House through the dark, rain started to fall again. The headlamps silvered the descending veils: the windscreen wipers clicked and swept softly. Viola said: 'Do you remember us visiting school once? My father and I at a half-term.'

'No,' said Garner, thinking hard. 'I'm afraid I don't.'

'You must have been about thirteen.'

'What eras ago,' said Garner. 'But I think now I do very vaguely remember it.'

'It was a summer term. I'd been off school with scarlet fever – that was why I was able to come. You came out to lunch with us on the Sunday at the hotel.'

'The Seaborough Arms, I expect,' said Garner.

'After lunch my father went to sleep in the lounge and you, William, and I went on the beach. I was terribly impressed by your eating some cockles at a stall near the harbour.'

Garner was stirred by this evidence of his early genius. 'I certainly don't remember that,' he said. 'Did you and William have some too?'

'No,' she said, 'we just stood and watched you. Impressed but rather embarrassed.'

'I think the cockle stalls were out of bounds. I expect that accounted for my behaviour.' He thought that all through life one acted asininely, trying to impress one's character on the world.

'Afterwards,' said Viola, 'we went on the sandhills and played hide and seek.'

And now Garner really remembered: a girl in a short red spotted frock with whom he lay in a hollow of the dunes, their hands for a moment accidentally touching; the contact forgotten immediately afterwards in the interest of the game, but recalled poignantly after the gas had been turned out in the dormitory, a lost opportunity and pleasure which he had felt would never come again.

'I admired you very much,' she said. 'And for quite a long time afterwards.'

'We never met again,' said Garner, conscious that here was a moment in which the nature of time was made almost clear, whose elements he must be able to retain and reproduce on paper. It was this same body, this brain looking out on the lit, steely road with its black, shadowed ruts, that Viola had once touched and that had remembered.

'Until the other day,' she said.

'Not twenty,' said Garner, 'but thirty years after.' He

glanced surreptitiously at her profile, trying vainly to see in it the forgotten features of that young girl.

'It's when you can say "thirty years ago" that you really begin to realize how short life is,' she said sadly. 'I think life must seem shortest in one's forties, when youth is so many years away but before one has really changed.'

'The strange thing is', he said, battling with the difficulty of putting the idea into words, 'the thread that links people together. Sometimes it's so tenuous you might think it broken. But then the event proves it was there all the time. Millions of threads, umpteen to every person.' That was not quite what he meant. He started on another tack. 'Do you remember me as I was that half-term?'

'I did before I met you again.' She rubbed the condensation off the windscreen with the back of her black-gloved hand. 'Now the two images have run together.'

'It's the beard,' he said, stroking it. 'That's an image to block out any other.'

'Yes,' she said seriously. 'I'd like to see you without the beard.'

'The thirteen-year-old boy isn't beneath it, I assure you,' he said. He wondered if underlying her remark was the idea – so familiar to his private thoughts – that behind (or even *in*) his conventionally unhandsome appearance was something of extreme interest, even beauty. Yes, he thought, one is always desiring to be loved.

'How frightful I must have been at thirteen,' he went on 'A lump – a formless lump. I was a late developer.'

'No,' said Viola. 'We always looked on you with awe.'

He fell silent, pondering on her viewpoint, and the gulf between it and his honest view of himself.

In the dim light of the hall, when they had put the car away, she dropped her gloves, and as she bent to pick them up he saw the whiteness and shadow of her breast. With surprise he felt his senses respond, as a growing boy suddenly realizes the charms of an elder and long-known family friend.

'We'll sit in the dining-room,' she said. 'The fire will still be in.' And he perceived the new ambiguity in their relations, feeling the anxiety of one who does not know whether he is achieving the conduct expected of him. In the dining-room she stooped again, to open the doors of the slow combustion stove and to rake out the ashes, and the fire glowed on her skin. He knew how easily the wish found the opportunity to express itself through trivial gestures, and looked deliberately away to the table, the two hide chairs, the sideboard – where, he was touched to observe, had been set out a decanter of whisky and some tumblers.

Soon he was sitting in one of the chairs, sipping the whisky, sensing the quietness of the house, calculating with a mixture of anticipation and alarm the hours of intimacy which lay ahead. He put down his glass on the table at his side. 'This is good,' he said, and as the words came out he knew that he meant them.

Viola smiled. She was sitting in the other chair, and he saw in her attitude the small degree of relaxation that marked almost dramatically the growth of their familiarity. He wondered why she had never married; what obstruction existed in her psyche.

She said: 'William and I sometimes used to sit here in the evenings.'

'Yes,' he said, glancing down at the little table and remembering the night of insomnia when he had filched the bath olivers. 'I noticed that your books were here.' There was still Trevelyan's *English Social History*, but the novel, he seemed to think, had changed – now it was *The Ballad and the Source*. He held it up and asked Viola if she were reading it. She said she was and enjoying it very much. As he replaced it he saw that the book underneath was the pamphlet on *Maud*, borrowed from the London Library. 'Who's been doing some recherché research on Tennyson?' he asked.

'Oh, the little *Maud* book,' she said. 'It must have been William.'

Garner said: 'I didn't know he was a member of the London Library.'

'He wasn't. He must have borrowed it from someone. I don't know quite what to do with it.'

Something opened in Garner's mind and he saw the whole train of events – the mortuary, Kershaw, his journeys to Askington. 'I'm a member,' he said. 'I'll return it when I get back to town.' He picked the book up and slipped it in his side-pocket. 'And I'll find out the name and address of the person who had it out.'

She looked at him quickly. She said: 'Do you think . . . ?'

'It might be,' he said gruffly. The thought that at last he had found something practical to do for her was mixed with the not dissimilar thought of the ritual of going to bed: of the journey to the bathroom, of the chance of passing her in the half-lit corridors, of the secrecy of bedrooms. He tried to discover, through the slight numbness induced by the whisky and the hock, what he really wanted.

Chapter Seven

To Garner's surprise the coroner adjourned the inquest on Widgery after he had given evidence identifying the body. He shuffled out of the limelight to the chair in the front row of chairs on which he had left his hat and raincoat. He bent down for the canvas grip which he had had no time to leave anywhere since he came off the train. He straightened to find standing beside him the sallow detective, the senior of the two who had visited him in Bayswater.

'Can you spare a minute, sir?' asked this man. 'Chief Inspector White would like a word with you.'

Garner felt the blood rush to his cheeks. 'Certainly, certainly.'

The detective led the way out of the little courtroom, down the white-tiled passage to a room with the word 'Witnesses' on the door. A thick-set man wearing a black homburg was leaning against the mantelpiece knocking his cigarette ash into the old-fashioned grate.

'This is Mr Garner, sir,' said the detective. The thick-set man said how d'you do, and shook hands. They sat down at a deal table which was dark with the moons of inkbottles, innumerable fingers, cigarette burns.

'I'm going to be quite frank with you, Mr Garner,' said the Chief Inspector. 'We are puzzled about these two deaths.'

'Yes,' said Garner.

'You know about the death of this man Kershaw, of course. He was employed by Widgery's firm. Here we have two deaths, the first possibly suicide, the second apparently accidental. The two men are closely connected. We'd like to get to the bottom of it.'

'I don't think it has a bottom.' Then Garner added foolishly: 'It's like the tale of the tub.'

The Chief Inspector did not betray any amusement. 'Well, now,' he said, 'I don't know that we are very interested in what you *think*, Mr Garner. But I understand that you were just about the last person to see Kershaw alive.'

Garner felt as embarrassed and angry as when, at school, he had been rebuked by his contemporaries who had become prefects before him. 'The last person?' he repeated. 'Yes, I suppose I was.' He visualized the police inquiries at Cuffs and wondered what they were all thinking.

'Why did he come to see you?'

'I don't know,' said Garner. 'Perhaps he felt lonely in London.'

'Let me put it another way,' said Chief Inspector White, patiently. 'What did he talk to you about?'

'Widgery's sister thought I ought to have some support in this to-do of Widgery's death, so she sent Kershaw down. It wasn't necessary. She'd given Kershaw my address at Cuffs and so he came to see me there when he couldn't get me at home. We didn't talk about anything so far as I recall except what a frightful business it all was.' One had, really, to cooperate with the prefects.

'Did Kershaw seem worried about anything?'

'Well, he did say he thought he was being watched by you – the police. Was he?'

The Chief Inspector ignored the question. 'Where had he been watched?'

'I think he said on the train from Askington. And coming to see me at Cuffs.'

'He was in a nervous state?'

'No, I wouldn't say that.'

'But he was concerned to think that the police were keeping him under observation?'

'Naturally.'

'Where was he going when he left you?'

'He didn't say.' Garner thought 'The Windmill Theatre,' but resisted uttering it.

'Now, Mr Garner, you're an intelligent man. What conclusion have you come to about the affairs of Widgery's firm?'

'As far as I know it's all right.'

'You've just come back from Askington?'

'Yes.' Garner was astonished that his activities should be a matter of common knowledge.

'Did anything happen there which might throw any light on this affair?'

Garner shook his head. He thought of himself and Viola, and how motives, unsuspected, grew out of events. And he became aware of a man in the corner of the room who seemingly was taking down all he said. The lower half of the wall was painted chocolate, the upper half bile: a thick black line divided the halves. He was beginning to dislike this interview. In the moment when the Chief Inspector glanced inquiringly at the sallow detective, Garner said: 'Shall I be wanted for the inquest on Kershaw?'

'No,' said the Chief Inspector, 'I don't think so. His brother has identified the body. But of course we might want you to help us if some more facts come to light. So if you are going out of London, let us know.' The Chief Inspector stood up. Garner was dismissed.

Cramming his hat on as he walked down the corridor encumbered with raincoat and hold-all, he suddenly remembered Rogers, stopped, and half turned back. Did the police know about Widgery's affair? That was one thing Kershaw had talked about in Cuffs – and his intention of 'telling all'. But blow the police. He turned and walked out into the patchy sunlight and whirling dust of the mean street. It was perhaps rather strange that apart from that oblique reference over the *Maud* pamphlet he and Viola had never again discussed Rogers. Did they both take it for granted that Widgery had committed suicide for love of that young man? And that Garner's task was some private administration of justice, demanding God knew what qualities of courage and power?

And, of course, he had never told Chief Inspector White about Kershaw's self-confessed interest in Widgery's death.

Over a cup of tea in an Express Dairy Garner tried to recover the normal tempo of his life. He took out his notebook and unscrewed his fountain-pen, but these gestures no longer seemed to have meaning. He put the things away and inhaled the steam of his tea, staring into the distance. It was 4.30: at seven o'clock he had a long-standing engagement to speak at the Centre of Contemporary Culture. He decided that he had time to go to the London Library. He drained his cup, recovered his hat, hold-all, and raincoat, and thought how glad he would be when the pubs opened and he could take the edge off his weariness. He saw clearly how one became a boozer.

It was as he turned off Jermyn Street into Duke of York Street and stopped for a moment at the open window of the newsagent's shop to buy the *New Statesman* that he thought someone was following him. A man behind him had crossed the road and stood looking in the window of Herbert Jenkins: a man wearing a navy-blue raincoat or overcoat – Garner could not bring himself to turn his full gaze on the figure. Garner ostentatiously read his copy of the *New Statesman* as he walked down to St James's Square and turned right past Chatham House. He tried to think what there had been in his interview with Chief Inspector White that would make the police put a man on his tail.

At the top of the steps of the Library he pushed the door as he always did instead of pulling it, and while he fumbled he contrived to look back into the square. A few people were apparent among the parked cars but none of them was near. Garner went through the doors and up to one of the ladies sitting at the 'in' counter.

'Excuse me,' he said. 'I happen to have found a book belonging to the Library. I wonder if you could tell me easily who took it out?'

He had imagined that all that would be involved was a quick visit to the mysterious regions at the back of the entrance hall. But the lady looked puzzled.

'You are a subscriber?' she asked.

'Yes,' said Garner. 'But this isn't one of the books I've taken out myself. It's one that seems fortuitously to have come into my possession and I wondered whose it was.' He felt himself getting red: he should have come armed with a better story.

'Oh, I see,' said the lady. 'But I'm afraid we aren't allowed to disclose the names of subscribers. Of course, if you let me have the book we will ensure that the subscriber is advised that it has been returned to the Library.'

Garner was flummoxed. 'You *can* tell from your records, though,' he said, 'the name of the member who has a particular book out if one simply gives the name of the book.'

'Certainly, if there is only one copy of the book in the Library.' The lady looked at Garner rather oddly. 'But it is a strict rule that we mustn't divulge the member's name.'

'Yes,' said Garner. 'I appreciate that.'

'Have you the book with you?'

Garner's cheeks were burning. 'No, I haven't.' He could not leave behind an impression of complete dottiness. 'As a matter of fact,' he added, laughingly, 'I haven't *really* found a book belonging to another subscriber. I'm working out the plot of a murder story. I thought perhaps I could have a London Library book for a clue.'

'Oh, I see,' said the lady, dubiously.

'The amateur detective finds the book at the scene of the crime, gets the name of the man who borrowed it from the Library, and so is led to a vital witness. Only now I see that it wouldn't work.'

'No,' said the lady.

'Ah well,' said Garner. 'I must try to devise another clue. A pity.' He smiled ingratiatingly. 'So sorry to have wasted your time.'

'Oh, that is quite all right,' said the lady.

'Thank you,' said Garner, shuffling awkwardly away. 'Thank you very much.' As he escaped up the main staircase John Foster's clock tinkled out five o'clock. He would, he thought, have to return the bloody thing anonymously by post – and tell Viola of his ignominious defeat. And the Library had now become just one more place where he had reason for embarrassment, a metaphorical restaurant in which he had vomited.

On his way up to the Literature section he called in at the gentlemen's lavatory. He stood in the dark, single urinal, the acrid smell of the temple of Jupiter Ammon in his nostrils, and thought as he always thought what a splendid setting it would make for a Graham Greenesque spiritual crisis. Or the dumping ground for a body in a detective novel. And then he remembered the sense of pursuit he had had in Duke of York Street, and the hair-shirt of worry tickled him again.

He tried to reason clearly just why the police might be concerned about his movements, but the whole sequence of events since Widgery's disappearance seemed to lie under a fog of inexplicitness. Life was simply not like a detective novel: motives were not clear, events had not a single cause, things did not wholly explain themselves. And then, as usual, he looked into his own mind for the explanation.

Obviously, he was not in fact being followed: the dark figure opposite the Ladies' Turkish Bath was a product of his own sense of guilt. The Eumenides had no reality. He thought of his ambiguous relationship with Viola: the quietness, the increasing intimacy, the opportunities presenting themselves successively and his rejection of them one by one until his nerves were in shreds and he had been condemned to another sleepless night in that house. Had she been awake too? He shuddered at his inadequacies, and longed for the privacy and absorption he could find only in his own rooms, his own contrived life.

He emerged from the lavatory, continued up to Literature, found Humphry House's *The Dickens World*, and came down the stairs again. While he was here, he thought, he might as well get the Bernard Van Dieren book. He was toying with the idea of writing an essay on Busoni, an essay that he might print in *Light*. He turned into the twilight of the rooms on the first floor and looked for the Music shelves. Here, only thick iron grids divided the rooms from the floor beneath. As he wandered along, switching the section lights on and off, he became aware that underneath someone else was walking, following a parallel course. He stopped dead in the alley of books: in the comparative quiet that followed he heard a clank or two from the shoes of the man below on *his* grids, and then there was complete silence. At the Music shelves Garner crouched on his haunches, trying to peer, as he searched for *Down Among the Dead Men*, through the interstices of the iron floor. He was certain that somebody was down there, but that person could scarcely be looking for a book, for all was in darkness.

Garner found his book and stood up. The light he had switched on illuminated only a short section of the alley. On either side of him the tall shelves stretched into the increasing gloom. He felt a sudden compression in his chest, and an accession of childish fear. His hand hovered over the switch and then, with a wry gesture of concession to his folly, he left it on and walked back towards the main staircase.

He could not be sure whether or not he could hear those other footsteps. Perhaps there was some echo from his own. It was very late: the Library would shut at half-past five. In a momentary flurry of panic Garner wondered if it were not already that time, if the Library had not already closed its doors and left him marooned. He stopped again,

123

switched on a light, and looked at his watch. It was 5.14. He pretended to examine the books on Medicine, straining his ears for sounds from below. And then he thought, with a clarity and conviction that brought him out in a sweat, that the police would never follow him *into* the Library: they would simply wait for him in that ideal waiting-place, St James's Square. The doppelgänger underneath was someone who wished to harm him. As Widgery and Kershaw had been harmed, physically, cruelly.

Cunningly, his face taking on unconsciously an animal's expression, Garner walked without a sound *away* from the main staircase into the back store, and then tiptoed down two flights of wooden steps into the History basement. He came up another flight to the ground floor, and burst out, like a child from a dark corridor, into a lighted and populated room, into the main hall. It was almost with astonishment that he found everything normal – a bearded member glancing through the new foreign language books in one of the cases in the middle of the floor, a member wearing a clergyman's collar having his books entered.

As his own books were being entered Garner kept looking back to the main staircase, but no one emerged from it. Really, he thought, his nerves were in extremely poor shape. He promised himself an early night: a long read in bed with the Dickens book and Van Dieren, a beaker of Ovaltine, and four aspirins.

But when he stood up to deliver his lecture the feeling of unease returned. The Centre of Contemporary Culture occupied several first-floor rooms in the Brompton Road: the largest was given over to meetings and recitals. To-night it was full, but Garner felt no sense of gratification.

As he spoke he tried to look along the rows for a man in navy blue. A figure near the front wearing a duffle coat dyed that significant colour scarcely qualified: he had long hair and carried a copy of the Marx-Engels correspondence. But there was also a person at the back who did not appear to have any companion and whose dark-blue raincoat was unbuttoned to reveal a sober dark-blue suit. Of course many had removed their coats and put them under their seats.

'I hope I have shown', Garner was saying, 'by that brief discussion of Godwin's *Caleb Williams* and those early novels by Bulwer Lytton, that the novelist's rebellion in the industrial age was first expressed by making the hero a criminal. He was either a pseudo-criminal like Caleb Williams – a man hounded unjustly by society : or he was a true criminal like Lytton's Paul Clifford – but sympathetically drawn. Obviously, the symbol could not be carried too far: the true criminal had to be condemned morally. But he is shown to be bad because society is bad – and sometimes simply because he is against society he acquires virtue.

'And then, as industrial society shows its great strength, the criminal becomes too dangerous a figure for the novelist to sympathize with. He gets changed to the private detective. The private detective is on society's side but he still retains sufficient freedom of action to be posed not only against the anti-social elements the police cannot reach, but against the police themselves. The private detective's solution may be to punish the notorious blackmailer and let the obvious murderer go free. You can see the dichotomy in Raffles and in American crime novels. In the younger American society the detective is always being confused with the criminal, accused of the crime, by the official police.

'In the end, when the novelist's rebellion is weakest – indeed, non-existent – the private detective and the policeman merge into one figure: Inspector Roderick Alleyn, for example, and Inspector Appleby.'

Garner coughed and glanced down at his notes. He felt that he was wandering away from his subject which was 'Godwin to Greene: the Novel of Pursuit', a talk he had given several times before and therefore was rather blasé about. He changed his tack.

'Even in *Caleb Williams*, right at the beginning of the *genre*, there is that lack of seriousness that shows so obviously in our own times. Godwin was determined to write a story that would, as he said, "constitute an epoch in the mind of the reader". But when the book was finished he asked himself what he had actually done and was forced to admit that he had only "written a book to amuse boys and girls in their vacant hours". In other words, there is, in Godwin's conception and execution of *Caleb Williams*, a writing-down – as there is in the work of all novelists who have chosen to write an "entertainment" instead of a fully-felt novel. All novelists – from Godwin, through Stevenson, to Graham Greene.'

Garner looked at his wristwatch, which he had taken off and put next to his notes. He was ploughing through the talk too quickly: he had better spend a bit more time on *Caleb Williams*.

'Nevertheless *Caleb Williams* has the power that all good novels have to make us see beyond and beneath the ordinary events of life – to make us see what forces people to behave as they do and to what their behaviour is leading.

In *Caleb Williams* the pursued hero is the victim of his fellow man – man "dressed in the gore-dripping robes of authority", in Godwin's melodramatic phrase. And it is this battle with Things As They Are – that was the book's sub-title – that leads the hero to his sad ironic conclusion: "My life was all a lie".'

As he uttered these words Garner was seized with a sense of unhappiness – seized and without the opportunity of tracking the cause of the feeling down. He had to pour a drink of water from the carafe on the table to cover up the involuntary jam in his flow of words.

During the interval Garner stayed in his seat. Someone brought him a cup of dark watery coffee which had slopped and partially soddened the two Marie biscuits reposing in the saucer. A girl came up and shyly asked him to autograph a copy of *Goats and Compasses:* his pleasure in doing so was lessened by the fact that she was not pretty.

His chairman, who sat beside him – a Professor Pedley – said: 'A most interesting dissertation, Mr Garner. I really must look at *Caleb Williams*. Can it be easily got?'

'Not very easily,' smiled Garner. 'Don't think it's been reprinted since about 1902.'

'Indeed,' said Professor Pedley. 'Now why don't you ask the Everyman people to do it?'

'Mm,' said Garner. 'I suppose they might be interested.'

'Undoubtedly,' said Professor Pedley. 'Especially with the *cachet* of an introduction from your pen.'

Pedley had white hair and a red face: he moved in advanced circles without being advanced himself. He sucked at his pipe and added: 'This Graham Greene fellow – what do you really think of him?'

Garner tried to make a choice of all the ideas which

sprang up in his mind – prose style, religiosity, ignorance of people and affairs – but before he could say anything Pedley went on: 'I must say I don't make much of him myself. Perhaps I'm old-fashioned, but when I read Graham Greene I can't help saying to myself "Life simply isn't like this". Now I don't say that when I read Trollope, though you and I know how much Trollope leaves out.'

Garner quickly adapted himself to the level and said: 'Yes, I see what you mean. The Greenish things just don't happen to one, do they? The terror in the public lavatory, the spiritual crisis on Clapham Common – it's too much.'

'Too much,' said Professor Pedley. 'We *are* civilized, you know: there *is* an order in human affairs. This happens' – he waved his pipe to indicate the chattering audience, the chink of cups, the tobacco smoke – 'and there's nothing sinister about it. No modern Moriarty behind it, stretching out his tentacles . . .' Pedley laughed his hard laugh.

'No,' said Garner. 'I hope not, anyway.'

His flat that night, after his day and a half's absence, added to its virtues the beauty of unfamiliarity. He had come straight home after the lecture, without dining, remembering an unfinished loaf and his untouched cheese ration. In his post was a letter from Hargreaves, Son and Mason, a firm of solicitors in Askington. It was headed 'William Widgery deceased', and the word seemed to change that dreamlike experience in the mortuary to an irrevocable historical state that sent a crepitation over his flesh. 'We have been instructed', said the letter, 'by Miss Viola Widgery to act for her and you in connexion with the estate of the above-named deceased, and have pleasure in enclosing a copy of the will for your information. We are preparing the necessary papers to lead to grant of probate, and will write to you again in due course.'

Garner looked with curiosity at the will. His own name leapt out at him: it was like reading an article that, half to one's astonishment, mentioned one's work. 'I bequeath to the said George Garner the sum of £500 free of duty.' Garner's eyes filled with tears.

The will was surprisingly long. There was a bequest to Viola of Widgery's shares in Widgery Bros. Ltd, and a legacy of £100 to Kershaw. There was a rigmarole about selling, calling in, and converting into money Widgery's estate, and extensive provisions defining the power of investment. There was a clause bequeathing patents and interests in patents to the trustees, and giving them power to grant licences for manufacturing the subject-matter of such patents in consideration of royalties to be paid to the trustees, and a direction about treating a proportion of the royalties as capital. It was quite a while before Garner found the kernel of the will: so far as he could interpret the jargon Viola had half the residuary estate absolutely and a life interest in the other half. On her death the capital of the latter half was to be divided among a number of charities. One of them was the National Cancer Research Foundation, and in this case Widgery had expressed a wish that, if practicable, his bequest should be used to build and equip a laboratory to be known as the Elizabeth Widgery Laboratory – a pious gesture to his mother's memory, perhaps. Evidently Widgery had been richer than his modest style of life suggested.

As Garner took off his jacket and tie and put on a filthy,

worn, camel-hair dressing-gown he could not help thinking about what he should do with his £500. He read *Down Among the Dead Men* over his meal and then sat smoking, his notebook on his knee, the gramophone playing Beethoven's Opus 131 quartet.

When the curtain rose on the Busoni opera, he thought, it revealed another curtain. The second curtain rose on a puppet show. It was the grotesqueness and cruelty of puppets that Busoni saw as final reality: as well (Garner guessed) as their raw simplicity and symbolism which had fascinated him throughout his life. And yet (or, rather, because of that) Busoni's masterpiece lacked genius: it was merely *about* genius.

Artists of the second class knew all the rules for being a genius, but missed the final absorption in, acceptance of, life: they preferred art. Busoni once said about Beethoven: one would often like to ask why you are in a bad temper. That was to see things too clearly, just as he saw too clearly to be able to compose it the kind of music the times required. And then Busoni really despised the means of music – he wanted a piano with eight octaves or two manuals, and wrote a set of fugues for no particular instrument. Beethoven came to reject all means except the string quartet but he exploited that vehicle, respected it, and made even its elementary resources serve his advanced purposes.

The ringing of the telephone made Garner jump as though a pistol had been fired behind his chair. He switched off the gramophone and picked up the receiver.

'George? This is Roderick Fox.'

'Hello, Roderick. How are you?'

Fox brushed this foolish question aside. 'George.' The

voice had assumed its brisk, businesslike manner. 'I've been trying to get hold of you since yesterday.'

'Ah,' said Garner. 'I've been away.'

'I hope you can manage this, George,' said Fox, severely. 'Perrott wants us to have dinner with him tomorrow.'

'Saturday?' said Garner, dubiously.

'Yes,' said Fox. 'I know it's short notice now, but I think we ought to make an effort.'

'All right.'

'Splendid,' said Fox. 'Seven-thirty at Perrott's house. He lives in St John's Wood. 9 Temple Gardens. Have you got it?'

'Yes,' said Garner, pulling the telephone pad towards him.

'I look forward to seeing you, George.'

'Yes,' said Garner, gnomically. Fox rang off.

Perrott's name broke Garner's dream of the previous night at Askington. He had dreamed of a situation in which he had deserted his wife for Sarah Freeman – a painful situation, because he had felt many bonds between his wife and himself and only an irrational, stupid desire for Sarah. In the dream his wife was not Victoria but Viola.

He stood by the telephone in a trance, tracing some of the complicated allusions of the dream. By comparison, he thought, the analysis of even an obscure poem was simple. Some years before his wife had left him he had had a love affair during which, for a while, he had half-seriously envisaged leaving his wife. It was the emotional tone of that episode which had attached itself to the dream. The substitution of Viola for Victoria was not simply the dream's pun or verbal slip: he saw that his relationship with Widgery's sister could stand for the relationship he might have had now with Victoria. For it was almost eight years since he and Victoria had parted and she must be forty-three. They would have slipped imperceptibly into the ease and acceptance of middle age, the initiative would have passed to him, and he would have been compensated for the years he had suffered.

He undressed and made himself some Ovaltine. Before he got into bed with it he switched out the light and peeped through the curtains into the square. The few lamps lit up, unnaturally green, patches of swaying trees. The square seemed to be deserted. Was it only the night of insomnia which had caused him to start so violently at the sound of the telephone?

And Perrott. The man was going to be a nuisance if he imagined that his money gave him the right to insist on literary dinner-parties.

Chapter Eight

'AM I too early?' the girl asked.

'No,' said Garner. 'Come in. I'm late this morning. Overslept.' Overslept was the wrong term, since he hadn't slept at all until after half past four. But his irritability dispersed a little now that a third person was here and he was prevented from brooding about his health. He poured himself another cup of tea and put it on the mantelpiece. 'You can take the dishes away, Marjorie.'

'Mother says these belong to you,' said the girl. 'The postman pushed them through our door this morning.' She held out some letters.

'Thank you,' said Garner.

'Did you see the man who called here yesterday?' asked Marjorie.

'What man?'

'A man stopped me on the steps yesterday afternoon and asked me which was your flat.'

'What was he like?'

She considered. 'Not young. False teeth, I think. He wasn't a Londoner. He had a northern voice – might have been Scottish.'

So the doppelgänger had a form. 'What else did he say?'

'Nothing much. He wouldn't leave his name. I said I could give you a message, but he said it didn't matter.'

'What time was this?'

'I don't know exactly. Was it something important?'

'No,' said Garner. 'No. I don't expect so.'

Her eyes, roving about aimlessly and without effect,

gave her personality qualities of remoteness and relative unimportance, as though she were an animal. Because she could not see him, Garner was constantly tempted to overact to himself his feelings. He finished his tea as though it were the last drink of one about to cross the Sahara.

Marjorie went into the kitchen with the crockery and Garner looked at his letters with a distraught eye. There was one from Viola Widgery. He put it at the back of the pile, like a worrying thought. But at last he had to open it, and to admit as he did so the possibility of her making demands of him. He did not know whether he feared or desired them.

She had, however, written only a few businesslike lines:

'I thought you ought to know immediately that I went back to the mill this morning and spoke to David Knowles, the young boy who used to tidy up William's laboratory. He is a bright lad, but has had no training and knew nothing of what went on in the laboratory. I asked him if William had ever spoken to him about his work in the laboratory or if he had noticed anything unusual in recent weeks. He said, quite of his own accord, that he thought that some of the files which contained the laboratory records had gone from the shelf. He had first noticed this round about the time William went away. Of course he may have wanted to connect the two things or may be mistaken, but . . .'

By the callboxes at Marble Arch was a patch of dried vomit – a sure sign that the carefree and prosperous weekend had arrived. Garner's decision to use a callbox for his deception was a refinement which had somewhat allayed his uneasy sense of wrongdoing. He inserted his money, dialled the number, and, as soon as the ringing tone stopped, pressed Button A as though it were connected to a charge of dynamite.

'Is that the London Library?' asked Garner.

'Yes.'

'This is Brixton Police Station, Sergeant Jones speaking. A briefcase has been handed in here, found in Clapham Common Road. The contents afford no means of identifying the owner, except that they include a book from your Library. Now I wonder if you could give me the name and address of the person who has taken this book out?'

'Certainly, Sergeant. What is the name of the book?'

'*Tennyson's " Maud" Vindicated*.'

'And the number on the back of the title page?'

Garner fumbled in his pocket for the book, and gave the number.

'Just hold on a moment or two, please.'

It was too easy. As he waited he foolishly and apprehensively looked round through the glass of the callbox for an approaching policeman. But what could he be charged with, anyway? In the mirror on the wall of the box he saw his face reflected in a flattering light, the skin almost tanned, the eyes sparkling. Well, he could survive successfully two putrid nights: now that he knew that his features did not show them he felt almost stimulated by them. Sensitive, suffering, unlike other men, but capable of revealing and interpreting their real desires.

'Hello,' said the voice on the other end of the line. 'Sorry to have kept you waiting so long.'

'That's all right, miss,' said Garner. He felt pleased with his acting.

'The book was taken out by Mr Peter Rackham. His address is 14 Winsome Street, S W 3.'

'Thank you very much. That's very helpful. I'm much obliged.'

'Not at all.' The voice was laden with complacent good citizenry.

He had set off, he realized, as they circled Sloane Square, thick with Saturday-morning shoppers, without any clear idea of what was going to happen. Why was he on the bus, anyway? He watched the striped awnings of Peter Jones slip by as in a dream, borne on to an obscure and unwished fate. This inexplicit action of death and alien desires had somehow multiplied to include himself, and his uneasiness grew to a schizophrenic crisis. As the bus passed the barracks he stood up and walked down the aisle with the intention of getting off and returning to his own life. When the conductor looked at him he changed his mind and feigned ignorance. 'We're not at Chelsea Town Hall yet?' He sat on the edge of a seat near the platform and pretended to an interest in the unfolding King's Road.

Peter Rackham. This was obviously the elusive Philip Rogers. Garner tried to remember what Viola had said about him. And, what was more important, he tried to think of an approach – something that he might say as, like a brush salesman, he stood on the threshold of 14 Winsome Street, facing this figure whose yellow hair was the only thing about him with any definition.

Winsome Street was a short road of cottage properties parallel with the King's Road: a few brightly-coloured front doors showed the extent of artistic penetration. Garner rang the bell of number 14. He found that his mouth was dry, his feet fidgety. He could not justify to himself his status in this affair; he feared that this man would simply look blankly at him and shut the door rudely. As he waited he tried in vain to see what lay behind the curtains of vermilion hessian that masked the front-room window.

The door opened to disclose the figure of Sarah Freeman.

Garner's astonishment was too great to permit him to observe whether she, too, was astonished. For a thunder-struck moment he tried to find a gesture, a word, that would conceal his emotion. Then his hand went up and he removed his hat: in that instant of time he restored his faculties to some sort of balance, and discovered a formula, even though it was a slightly absurd one.

'Hello,' he said. 'I've come to find out why you abandoned me at that dreadful party.'

'George Garner,' she said, and then added: 'Come in.'

He sensed some circumstances behind her of inconvenience: a cake in the oven or a man in the bedroom. 'Is it all right?' he asked.

In the narrow hall she took his hat and put it on one of a row of hooks: next, he noticed, to a smart little hound's-tooth cloth cap. He remembered what during the last minute he had forgotten, that this was where Rackham lived. Did Sarah live here as well? And with Rackham? Or was she merely a visitor? It was like the probable improbability of a Dickens novel.

She said, answering one of his unspoken questions: 'How did you find out my address?'

They went into the sitting-room: the curtains had hidden a divan covered with more hessian, some furniture in chrome wood, a table lamp made out of a Chianti bottle, and a lithograph by William Scott.

'How did I find out?' said Garner, with hideous roguishness. 'Aha!'

She showed him into a chair and offered him a box of cigarettes. She stood stroking the plant on the mantelpiece and regarded him smilingly.

'No, seriously,' said Garner. 'I got it from what's-her-name.'

'Who?'

He could not remember the name: he felt perspiration in the creases of the hand that held the cigarette. 'You know,' he said. 'The party woman.'

'Minnie Cartwright?'

'The same,' said Garner. He blew smoke.

'Did you actually go to Highgate again?'

'Phoned her,' said Garner. He suddenly saw clearly that Sarah's smile was quite false, the smile, perhaps, of someone concealing a crushing headache. He felt a desperate desire to fill out the awful skeleton of the conversation. 'I've been away for a couple of days,' he said, 'or I would have inflicted myself on you before. I suppose it's I who ought to apologize for that night, really – for getting rather tight. It was that deceitful punch, I seem to remember. Do you know, I missed the last Tube and didn't get a taxi until I'd staggered to Euston.'

'How frightful for you,' she said.

There was a silence: Garner was almost impelled to break it by asking some meaningless question – 'Have you seen any good films?' or 'How often do you water your cactus?' Sarah still stood, now looking over his shoulder out of the window. The situation was ridiculous as well as

138

painful: he rose and said gravely: 'I think you'd like me to go, wouldn't you?'

Her expression became real. 'Of course not,' she said. 'Do sit down.' She sat down herself and left him stranded. He turned his back on her and went to the window.

'Where's Rackham?' he asked.

He heard her chair creak. She said: 'Who?'

'Rackham,' he said. 'Peter Rackham. He lives here, doesn't he?'

'Yes,' she said. Her face was scarlet.

Now that he saw that her armour was not impenetrable he became almost jovial. 'Don't be alarmed, my dear Sarah. I'm not going to serve him with a writ.'

'It was Peter you came to see, wasn't it?'

Garner failed to think of a reason why he should not tell her. 'Yes,' he replied. And then he added facetiously: 'But of course, now that I've found you . . .'

She almost stamped her foot. 'Oh, for God's sake!' She fumbled a lighter out of her skirt pocket. 'How did you know Peter lived here?' She reached across with shaking fingers and took a cigarette out of the box.

'Tut, tut,' said Garner. But he had frozen at the sound of the emotion in her voice.

She succeeded in lighting her cigarette. 'How did you know?' she repeated.

'I don't want to seem impolite' – on some syllables his voice trembled slightly – 'but is it any concern of yours?'

'Peter's concerns are mine.' She was like a schoolgirl confessing to save the class from detention, he thought. But in the middle of his other feelings – confused, bewildered feelings – he experienced a pang of unreasonable jealousy, and took in afresh her throat rising out of the oatmeal-coloured shirt, her nylon legs emerging from the brown and white checked skirt. Her clothes seemed an extension of her desirable flesh. In a curious way the pang reassured him: could there possibly be any concatenation of circumstances which would make it important for him to dissemble before her?

'Are you living with him?' he asked. His voice, he found, sounded detached.

'Yes,' she said, 'if that's any concern of yours.'

'You astonish me,' he said. 'I was given to understand that Rackham had other inclinations.'

She made no reply, so he ploughed on. 'It's quite a strange story,' he said. 'You might not even believe it. I found a book in the house of a gentleman friend of your gentleman friend, and –'

She said quickly: 'So it was the London Library book.'

'Yes, it was the London Library book,' he said, trying, like an amateur photographer, to accommodate her extra figure into the already overcrowded group. 'How did you know?'

With a violent gesture she threw the end of her cigarette behind the gas fire. 'You innocent,' she said. 'You innocent.'

Garner uncrossed his thick tweed legs and stared at her. Embarrassment overcame his anger and a boyish blush crept out of the roots of his beard. He opened his mouth, but could find nothing to say.

'What have you come here for?' she asked.

He had no other thought than to speak the truth. 'I don't know exactly. It's all rather complicated. I had a friend –'

She interrupted him again. 'Yes, yes. But what were you going to do with Peter?'

'Do with him?' Garner wiped some moisture off his forehead. 'Look, this is all too absurd. We're two civilized, ordinary people. Why can't you be frank with me? What is this all about?'

'You tell me.'

He saw almost with alarm that his appeal had not made the least impression on her. Perhaps there was only one civilized ordinary person, as he had so often painfully learned but never remembered. She gazed on him with a blank countenance. 'This friend of mine,' he said. 'I felt I had to find out . . .' And then he stopped and said: 'The London Library book. That was why I was followed. I *was* followed.'

'Why don't you forget about all this, George,' she said, as though humouring a fractious imbecile.

He tried to laugh and found himself tittering. 'It *is* absurd. Forget what? Your young man caused my friend's death –'

'Caused his death?' She looked round from the window to which she had walked after her last ingratiating question.

'Well, dragged him out of his settled little life – dragged him to London – goodness knows what.'

'Well, what?'

'I don't know,' said Garner. 'I suppose that's what I came here to discover.' And he repeated to himself the question for Rackham which he had laboriously formulated as though it were the possible key to a lock of whose interior he was ignorant: When were you last with Widgery?

'I think you ought' – Sarah was looking out of the window again – 'I advise it for your own good – to tell me just what you've discovered in this – affair.'

'What melodrama!' he said. But really he was beginning to find the situation not melodramatic: it was all too disturbingly normal. And he did not like her preoccupation with the window. 'Obviously we're at cross-purposes, my dear Sarah. I think I had better go.' He rose. 'One thing puzzles me. Just what did Rackham hope to gain by – er – shadowing me?'

'It wasn't Peter,' she said.

'It wasn't?' he echoed, stupidly.

'What on earth induced you to mess about with this business? What did you think you could do?' A thin strand of hair had fallen over her brow, like the first tiny fault in a neat elaborate machine doomed to a spectacular seize-up. 'The man who followed you was called Trimmer. Forbes Trimmer. Ever heard of him?'

'No.'

'I think he was once middleweight champion of the Army. But he put on a lot of weight in the Isle of Man during the war. I thought you might have known him because in the thirties, when he was a steward at a Mosley meeting, he nearly killed a man. You were rather political in those days, weren't you?'

Garner did not reply. She went on: 'Now if you'll confide in me, George –'

He said: 'I really don't want to hear any more. I must go.'

'Don't be a b.f., George. You can't just walk out of it.'

He was at the door. 'Are you going to try to stop me?' He had a quick satisfying vision of smashing his fists into her, kicking himself free as she grasped his legs.

'I can't stop you,' she said, following him into the little hall.

'Of course you can't.' He reached for his hat. 'I've never heard such nonsense in my life. This is England.' He even had the control to smile to himself at the curious instinct that had brought out that last remark from the depths of his conditioning.

'The trouble with you', she said savagely, 'is that you've never lived.'

He felt as though she had hit him across the face. Without a word he put on his hat and opened the door. Halfway up the short garden path was a young man, hatless, in a cream turtle-neck sweater and nigger-brown worsted trousers. Garner walked towards the gate and made a sort of obsequious obeisance and a polite detour so that the young man would pass him. But the young man stopped. Sarah said from the front step: 'Do you know Mr Garner, Peter?'

'Yes,' said Peter Rackham. 'I have that pleasure.'

Garner's hands and thighs were trembling uncontrollably. 'I'm afraid I don't know you,' he said in a voice that came shrill and thin. But as he said this and glanced up at the young man he saw that he did know him. The young man's hair would have been lemon-coloured had it not been cropped in a crew-cut: incredibly enough he was the young man of the Cartwrights' party.

'Come in and have a drink,' said Peter Rackham.

'Impossible,' muttered Garner. 'I'm late already.' He felt Rackham's hand grasp his upper arm, the brush of an alien world.

'Just a quick one,' Rackham urged, 'before lunch.'

'No,' said Garner. 'No.' And reckless, finally, as to the

143

proprieties of ordinary existence, he shook off Rackham's bony hand, ran into the street, and walked rapidly towards the safety of the King's Road. As he walked, his face on fire, his thoughts like some menacing insects roaring round his head, he felt as though he had come, shaken but alone again, out of a nightmare.

Chapter Nine

THE old man opposite ate his lunch wearing his battered grey homburg and a wrinkled raincoat of that grey-streaked black material that one sees worn by old men but never for sale in the shops. He had no teeth, so that with every bite his face collapsed like that of an indiarubber doll.

'I always have the curry when it's on,' he said to Garner. 'When my wife was alive she used to make a very good curry.'

Garner grunted, pushed away his unfinished plate, and pulled his coffee towards him.

'Isn't the vegetable hot-pot very nice?' asked the old man, solicitously.

'I'm not hungry,' said Garner.

'Sometimes it isn't very nice,' said the old man. 'I *have* tried it when the curry's been off. Although in that case I usually go for the shepherd's pie. I have to keep to something soft, you know, because of my teeth.'

Garner made no reply to this: he was looking past the old man's head, scrutinizing all the customers in turn, wondering whether he had been mad to come in this cafeteria, so near Winsome Street. But it was reassuringly crowded and so was the King's Road outside – crowded with people living normal lives, who knew that nothing terrible could happen to them.

'Of course,' said the old man, 'I never used to go into cafés when my wife was alive. It makes a lot of difference when your missis passes on. Are you married, may I ask?

'Yes,' said Garner, and then added quickly: 'No.' No, I am quite alone, he thought, with great self-pity.

'Ah,' said the old man, 'you ought to get married. But you artist chaps don't seem to settle down. All brain work.' He wiped his mouth with a handkerchief the colour and shape of a knob of pumice.

Garner was living over again, for the third or fourth time in the half-hour since they had happened, those events in Winsome Street. On each occasion his memory had, Wordsworthlike, recreated the original emotion, so that his thoughts were accompanied by a pounding of the heart, a frightful weakness in the marrow of his leg bones. Like a runner in some gruelling obstacle race, he toiled once more over the awful moments to that final one when he had shaken Rackham off, and then he sat back in his chair, breathing heavily, reaching out automatically and uncertainly for his cup. He tried to rationalize the situation, make it fit unobtrusively into the gentle circumstances of the rest of his existence. Of course, he said to himself, the plain fact is that this Rackham is a quite impossible figure and must be forgotten, ignored – he and his friends. His friends. What was the implausible name? Forbes Trimmer. Absurd, utterly absurd. And yet the vague shape that had lurked in Duke of York Street now had a name, a character, and a past. Again Garner looked anxiously through the lit haze of the cafeteria: looked for a navy-blue raincoat, a frame running to fat, the broken face of a boxer.

Then Garner, his thoughts revolving as in insomnia, so rapidly that he was unable to exhaust one subject before another rose up and pushed its predecessor away, tried to analyse the phenomenon of Rackham's presence at that party in Highgate. The fact that Rackham lived with

Sarah (Garner told himself reasonably) made it follow that he would know the Cartwrights and be invited to their house. There was no coincidence there. But why had Rackham and Sarah made their way to the party separately? They had obviously gone home together, leaving Garner to crawl drunkenly to Euston. Gone home together amused at that drunkenness and that abandonment.

It seemed to Garner that at that party he had talked volubly and freely to Rackham. But what about? His drunkenness blotted out the intimacy as effectively as the years that separate a school friendship from a casual meeting in middle life. If only he could remember, if he could have just a quiet few hours to arrange the whole affair in orderly sequence, if he could erase the pain and fear attached to it almost as irrationally as to an obsession! The train of his thoughts piled up again at that remark of Sarah's which he repeated to himself as though it were a memorable line of poetry: *The trouble with you is you've never lived.*

'Now I dare say you're a thinking chap.' Garner seized on the old man's words as one reads a brochure about Ramsgate in a dentist's waiting-room. 'I'd like you to accept this little pamphlet, *The Rule of Peace: When Will It Come?* There's no charge. Read it when you get home.'

'Thank you,' said Garner, stuffing the thing in his pocket and thinking that he daren't go home.

'It's the reign of the Devil and his crew we're experiencing now, you know,' said the old man. 'Wars, rumours of wars. You'll find it all in that little pamphlet. It's non-denominational, of course. We meet on Friday evenings in Glebe Place, just round the corner. Friends of Peace, we are. Everyone's very welcome.'

'I'm afraid I don't believe in the reign of the Devil,' said Garner.

'What else can you believe in these days?' asked the old man.

Garner considered. 'You've got a point there.'

'Course we have. It's all in the pamphlet. When my wife was alive I was like you – didn't worry my head about such things. But when you're alone you get thinking.'

'Yes,' said Garner.

'If it isn't the reign of the Devil, whose reign is it?'

Well, ultimately, reason prevails: reason and the ideals of art. But Garner did not say this. He said: 'Goodness knows.'

Some of the Saturday-morning workers were still on their way home. Some of those with the morning off were still wandering about arm in arm with their wives, or pushing perambulators, or speaking harshly to their children. Garner, having left the old man busy with a plate of prunes and mock cream, stood for a moment at the entrance to the cafeteria looking about anxiously, and then slipped into the throng on the pavement. He found himself walking in the direction of the barracks but he had not the least idea of his immediate destination. Several times he glanced over his shoulder, pretending, when he saw nothing to alarm him, to be looking at a clock, or stepping back a few paces to gaze in a shop window as though to examine more carefully some article of which he had at first caught only a fleeting impression. In the sky the sun shone behind a thin mist of cloud like gauze.

Outside a bookshop there was a case of books on which was pinned a notice 'Half Marked Prices'. This time he retraced his steps with genuine intent. A faint warmth of pleasure penetrated his numb brain. His eyes passed methodically along the rows. His hand made an impulse to pick out John Freeman's biography of Melville, and then fell back: he did not really want that even at half-price. But a little later he did take down *The Romantic Agony*. Before he opened it he promised himself that he would buy it if the marking were ten shillings or less. The marking was twelve and six: he returned the book to its space.

While he was squatting on his heels to examine the bottom rows, he heard a voice above him say: 'Mr Garner, can I have a word with you?' It was a Newcastle voice, hoarse under the whining accent. He saw beside him a pair of blunt black shoes, the extremities of thick grey flannel trousers, and the skirts of a navy-blue raincoat.

Garner struggled to a standing posture. 'No,' he said, confusedly. 'No, it's impossible. I have to –' And without making himself any more coherent he turned away from the unmoving figure at his side, turned away and walked back along the King's Road, walked rapidly and then, as the residual sense of shame disappeared, more and more rapidly, dodging between the passers-by, his head instinctively bowed as though to guard against a blow from behind. In that instant of turning he had caught a glimpse of a mottled face, greying eyebrows, but the features of his pursuer still remained otherwise a blank. He realized that not until this moment had he truly believed in that pursuer's existence – as a man will not believe that anything physically destructive can happen to him until the pain seizes him and he sees the changed world through hopeless eyes.

He looked along Oakley Street, saw that it held plenty

of people, and turned down it. A lorry overtook him and he suddenly remembered Kershaw's end. He hurried on, keeping close to the houses. He was starting to breathe heavily and there was a slight film over his eyes. He began to think of what he should do. To go to his flat was impossible: it was known, quiet, vulnerable. Cuffs were closed by now. But he must telephone Chief Inspector White: to no one else would his fear make sense. When he had thrown off this thing, this Trimmer, when he had made a callbox a refuge, not a trap, he would telephone, end the whole business, and then forget it.

He crossed the street with a group of young men, and risked a glance back. He saw nothing. He slackened his pace a little, wiping his sweating hands on his jacket. But just why was he being followed? In order to be frightened, menaced. Why? Baldly, because he knew that Rogers was Rackham. But to tell the police, to ask for protection, how would that save him from Trimmer? Rackham had put Trimmer on to try to prevent Garner discovering his identity, and when that failed, to work on him anyway. The flame of alarm in Garner's bowels burned up again. Violence, violence: how he feared and hated it.

He stopped at a pillar-box on a corner, sidled behind it, and looked up the street. Fifty yards away on the other side the raincoated figure marched steadily towards him: it wore a light grey hat, the brim turned down all the way: it was thick-set and walked with a stick. Garner turned and made off, every now and then breaking into a sort of swinging trot. Two boys playing marbles in the gutter looked up and watched him approach. One of them said: 'In a hurry, mate?' When they were behind him Garner heard their derisive laughter.

But soon he found his progress impeded. The pavements became more and more crowded: in the road was a slow-moving line of motor-cars and bicycles. The crowds, mainly of men in groups of two or three, were going in his direction, walking purposefully but at ease. It was, Garner decided, some proletarian festival of entertainment. The dogs, perhaps, if the dogs ran on Saturday afternoon; or a football match – professional association football matches were, he knew, very popular affairs. Gratefully he fell into step with the mob, feeling protected and anonymous.

The crowd slowed up and quite suddenly became a queue. A man in the roadway called out: 'Official programme.' Garner, sandwiched between a bus conductor and two youths, had a moment of panic in which he felt himself caught in a snare. And then he began to understand how safe he was, and let himself be taken slowly forward to whatever boring or vulgar spectacle lay ahead. He peered out cautiously round the bus conductor, through the gaps in the phalanx, to watch for Trimmer passing along the road; but the minutes elapsed and no Trimmer came, and Garner's pulses subsided, the perspiration on his legs drying under the hairy tweed.

The queue approached an old man playing the waltz from *The Merry Widow* on a battered brass cornet. The youths at Garner's side began to whistle and hum the tune in hot rhythm: they wore shoes with enormously thick crêpe soles, and ties decorated with nude girls; their hair was long and brushed back behind the ears so that the two sides just met at the back of the head. The DA style of haircut, thought Garner contemptuously, remembering with pleasure that someone had once told him that District

Attorney was merely a euphemism for Duck's Arse. How could a world which produced these boys be capable of any amelioration? On the other side of the queue the cornet player's colleague, a noseless man, crept along shaking a little black bag of coins.

The queue turned at last into a cinder-laid space before high wooden hoardings, and, like a river reaching its delta, spread out into a number of thinner queues that stretched towards some narrow gateways. Notices said: 'TICKET HOLDERS ONLY', 'BOYS', 'ADMISSION TO GROUND 1/6'. In one of the streams Garner, his chin sunk on his tie, tried to make himself invisible. It was an association football match, clearly: he would go in the ground, filter through the crowd, and after a little time emerge from another gate. He was pleased with his plan. His toes curled against the bottom of his shoes in sympathy with his desperate desire for the queue to pass beyond the turnstile. As he came nearer to the entrance he saw at the side of it another notice which read: 'NO CHANGE GIVEN'. Anxiously he examined his money: he had two half-crowns, two sixpences, and four pennyworth of copper. No mathematics could get exactly one and sixpence out of that. A fresh worry added itself to his gnawing stomach. He looked round almost imploringly at the solemn, the chaffing, the all alien faces, and dared not ask for help.

It became his turn to squeeze into the aperture. He said to the dim figure behind the grille, in the Jamesian locutions which always came out when he was embarrassed, holding all his coins on his outstretched palm, that he had no change and was it possible nevertheless to enter. Without a word the figure took half a crown and gave him a shilling back. Tears came into Garner's eyes at the kindliness and malleability of humanity and its customs, and he pressed almost happily through the turnstile.

Inside, the people were moving across a further cinder space, and then up wide steps to the top of an embankment. There was a cheer from the crowd beyond and a sputter of applause. A man next to Garner said to his companion: 'They're out', and quickened his pace. Garner moved up the steps. At the top he looked back. Beyond the turnstiles there was still a thick conveyor belt of spectators. In front they were running towards the embankment: except one man who, having detached himself from the barrier, took his stick from under his arm, leaned on it, and surveyed the scene, his turned-down hat tilting backwards until Garner was sure that the eyes under it had met his own.

For a moment or two Garner held his gaze, the distance giving him the illusion of safety, as though the man had been an animal behind bars. And then, with a sinking heart, he turned and pressed through the standing figures on the embankment. Suddenly he found that he stood at one of the narrow ends of a rectangular arena. Far below, the playing pitch, a lurid green against the neutral stands and the blue-and-pink pointilliste blur of faces and bodies, was sprinkled with two sets of brightly shirted manikins. There was the curious odour of tobacco burning in the open air. Garner edged sideways into the thickest part of the crowd. The players were arranging themselves into a theoretical order: a regular constellation of blue shirts faced a mirror constellation of black-and-white-striped shirts. Between them a ball rested on the grass like some grotesque yellow bloom. The thin sound of a whistle came up. Slowly at first, and then gaining momentum like an explosion, the two constellations broke up into a confused, random pattern. The yellow flower was sliced diagonally, pushed past a black-and-white doll, and then projected in a low parabola far down the centre of the green-baize table. A *wooh*, delayed for a moment but rising quickly to a crescendo, as though caused by some enormous valves which had to warm up, came from the packed terraces and stands.

Garner arrived at another flight of steps: this led to a gangway far below, running across the banking. He went down between the massed people, hearing their groans and excitement as though the emotions came from another mode of existence – as one hears the cries of a sleeping companion's dreams. The gangway was not far above the playing pitch: the game moved towards Garner, and as he hurried along he saw the striped and blue counters enlarged to the size of men, men with tousled hair and recognizable features, with breathing chests, who called to one another anxiously and who had to strain with all their physical powers to achieve the patterns which from the heights above had seemed effortless and inhuman.

To Garner's alarm the gangway ended against a high iron fence: beyond was one of the covered stands in whose gloom an irregular but continuous succession of struck matches winked out from all quarters like a complicated system of signals. Garner looked round. The gangway was deserted but he dared not retrace his steps. Along the iron fence yet another stairway led to the summit of the banking. Garner toiled up it.

At the top he paused for breath. He had now come to the corner of the embankment furthest from the turnstiles through which he had entered the ground. He could see down and across the great cliff of heads from which smoke rose in the faint sunshine as though from a gigantic refuse dump. While he looked, the ball, far below, was volleyed towards the near goal and, as the crowd roared again, flashed over the white matchstick crossbar. The solid-looking cliff suddenly disintegrated where the ball entered it, the heads and bodies waved aside to admit it, making an aperture like the fronded mouth of some voracious under-water creature, half flower, half fish.

By Garner's side, frightening him with its suddenness, came the clanging of a bell wielded by a man wearing a blue beret and an expression of serious concentration. And, as though its raucous tones had announced him, at the bottom of the long flight of steps Trimmer appeared, like the familiar but always terrifying figure of a recurrent nightmare. Garner turned. The place instead of a way of escape had become the trap for which it seemed designed. Broad steps led down, away from the crowd: Garner was forced to take them. Towards the bottom the fence ended against a block of lavatories. It was possible to veer left, along a broad pathway at the skeleton back of the stand. The pathway seemed long, was deserted. The catches in his breath he could, if he wished, turn easily into sobs. He came to a flight of wooden stairs which led into the heart of the stand. He looked back: his pursuer had not appeared. He started up the stairs.

A man in a cloth cap hastened out of the recesses under the stand, holding a cup of tea, calling: 'Your ticket, please sir.'

'My friend behind has got them,' panted Garner over his shoulder, inspired, and laboured on.

'Wait a minute, please sir,' came the man's plaintive voice. He was handicapped by his cup.

'My friend behind,' called Garner again, but not caring whether the man heard or not. He ran up the last few steps and emerged again into the surf-like sounds of the crowd. Through the comparative gloom, beyond the stand's low, dark roof, framed by its pillars, he could see the field and the players below lit as brilliantly as a stage. He made rapidly along the gangway for the other end of the stand. Half-way, a second and shorter flight of steps providentially led the reverse way to the area in front of the stand. Through this area, sparsely populated with men smoking cigars, men wearing smart trench coats, girls in tweeds with pimpled escorts, Garner threaded his way, putting distance between himself and his vision of Trimmer arguing with the ticket collector. He came to another iron fence. There was a gate through it and beyond the gate a car park. Garner turned the handle of the gate. It was locked. His exultation turned to panic. He rattled the handle like a child shut accidentally in a dark room, looking fearfully over his shoulder.

A man appeared beside him and said: 'Do you want to go out, sir?'

'Yes,' said Garner, seeing suddenly the happiness given by a relenting fate. 'Yes, I do, please.'

The man produced a key, turned the lock, and opened the gate. 'You'll be coming back?'

'I think not,' replied Garner. 'Doctor. Urgent call.' And as he said this the laboured breathing in his chest that whistled and hurt seemed all at once virtuous, and he could believe that he was in fact on some skilful humanitarian errand.

'Hard luck, sir. Looks like a good game.'

Garner smiled ruefully, and with a final touch of genius

– the last line of a sonnet that miraculously rhymes and unfolds simultaneously an unguessed image – pressed half a crown into the man's hand.

Behind him the voice called out warmly: 'Thank you, sir. Much obliged. Good luck, sir.' Garner made a path through the maze of bumpers and came out between open gates, where the attendant looked at him but raised no question. Behind him the animal still roared and groaned in its great rectangular cage. At the end of the quiet street the world was going about its normal business. Garner hailed a passing taxi. 'The Passengers' Club,' he ordered. As they drove away he climbed on the worn leather seat, peeped through the rear window, and saw nothing to alarm him. He settled himself back in the corner and, with hands that trembled so much that he looked at them with detachment as though they were someone else's, took a cigarette out of its packet and fed it to his eager mouth.

The marble nymph that guarded the hall of the Passengers' failed to conceal with her ungraceful hand her rather grimy breasts. In the little glass-walled porter's office a man hurriedly swallowed a mouthful of jam tart and called out: 'Good afternoon, Mr Garner.' Garner said: 'Good afternoon, Fred,' and went automatically to the letter rack, looked under G, and then climbed the broad stairs to the library. Everywhere was deserted and the great portraits looked over Garner's head to some indefinable point in time and space. There was a faint smell of stale tobacco smoke, vegetable water, and floor polish. The library was a comparatively small room lined with dusty books which nobody ever took down. Garner went to a table in the window, removed a sheet of notepaper from the rack, and unscrewed his pen. 'My dear', he wrote: looked out for a minute over the cowls and skylights of the roofs, and then added 'Viola'.

'It seems a lifetime since I had your letter this morning. People often use such banal phrases, but I mean it. Such a strange thing has happened: my life has been altered through your brother's affairs.

'I think – no, I'm sure – that I must go to the police and tell them everything I know about William's infatuation for the man you know as Rogers. His real name, or the name he uses here, is Rackham. I'm afraid that in some way this man was concerned in William's death, and perhaps in Kershaw's death. There is another man – maybe a friend of Rackham's or someone Rackham has hired . . .'

Garner put down his pen. He felt very tired, and it seemed a gigantic and hopeless task to try to convey to Viola the atmosphere, the growing urgency, of the last two days. He rubbed his face with his two hands, and then took up his pen again.

'. . . of a type that can do nothing but harm, who is also involved. When I started this letter I meant to write down everything that had happened, however unclear it was to me. But now I feel that I can't write it, can only tell it to you when we meet. We must meet soon . . .'

As Garner wrote those last four words he felt a melting tenderness and at the same time a huge desire to resign his responsibilities, for sympathy, for admiration. The memory of a perfume came so vividly that the elusive odour seemed actually to be in his nostrils. It was a few seconds before he realized that the perfume was Sarah's Arpège; that the memory came from that ugly scene in the little hall. He finished his letter hurriedly, unsatisfactorily.

'I know you will believe that what I shall do will be for the best. I will write again very shortly. Yours ever, George Garner.'

He addressed the envelope, put the letter inside it, and then slipped it in his wallet. He had not yet made up his mind to send it. He sat on at the table for a few minutes, his mind a blank, sensing the club stretch solidly and silently around him. Then he went downstairs to one of the lavatories. In those grave marble-and-mahogany surroundings he washed so thoroughly that the act took on spiritual or psychological meaning. He combed his beard and hair before one of the mirrors. He was pale with weariness, but there was a vitality behind the pallor which pleased him. The image turned to show its half-profile and assumed the interest and impressiveness of the frontispiece to a biography. For an instant Garner stood outside himself and yet retained an awareness of his body, his looks, his mind, his whole individuality, which in the same moment took on a significance far beyond his ordinary sense of his existence. He did not fully return to himself until he was in the corridor outside.

In the office the porter was picking his nose. 'There isn't by any chance', asked Garner, 'a room going for tonight?'

'Yes, sir,' said the porter, concealing his picking hand under the desk. 'Colonel Lisby had to return to Bristol rather hurriedly, sir.'

'Excellent. Can I have it?'

'Certainly, sir. I'll put you down in the book.' The porter, having disposed of his treasure, laid his hand nonchalantly on the top of the desk. 'It's the little room at the end.'

'I know it. Thank you, Fred.' Garner bounded up the

stairs, feeling the triumph right down to his leg muscles. They would bloody well watch his flat in vain. He went into the lounge on the first floor, took the *Spectator* folder from the rack, and pressed one of the bells. One or two ancient members were dozing by the fire, but otherwise the big room was empty. When the steward came Garner said: 'Is it too late for tea?' The old man said: 'Of course not, sir. What would you like, sir? Some nice toasted scones?' 'Yes,' said Garner. 'And some fruit cake, if you can find any'. The pleasurable realization that he was ravenously hungry was like a double brandy before a fatal interview.

He was reading the book reviews over his final cup of tea when a tall figure folded itself into the other corner of the gargantuan black sofa. Garner started nervously, and then said: 'Hello, Philip. It's been a long time since I saw you.'

'You were so absorbed, George,' said the tall man, 'I was almost frightened to interrupt you.' He giggled. 'I've often wondered who one would find in the Passengers' at 5.30 on a Saturday afternoon.'

'Well,' said Garner, lapsing easily into the semi-facetiousness of his relationship with this man, 'evidently P. E. Clauson.'

Clauson said: 'George, have a drink instead of that tea.' He pressed the bell on the wall above the sofa. 'I've an excuse for being here – I've been to Charing Cross seeing Fanny off to Folkestone. She has a concert there tomorrow afternoon. But your presence, George, is sheer eccentricity.'

How strangely Philip Clauson had changed! Garner thought. In spite of the missing button on his jacket, the great hole in his sock, an aura of calm domesticity surrounded him, almost an aroma of diapers. The buxom Fanny, in the intervals of singing the high parts in oratorio, had given him three – or was it four? – children. And though the face was still haggard, the nose hooked and all bone, Clauson had put on weight round the hips: and the once-abundant hair rose rather wispily from his skull and was no longer all gold. He chattered on.

'What's this I hear about a new magazine, George?'

Garner blushed. Clauson was one of those who had not received the initial letter asking for contributions. Garner told him about *Light*. He added: 'Of course, I want something from you, Philip.'

Clauson giggled again. 'Are you sure? I can never make up my mind whether you approve of me or not these days.'

Garner made a reassuring noise. The gins arrived and Clauson immediately slopped his on his trousers. Typical, thought Garner, and yet behind the clumsy, rather simpering person was a mind hard and quite acute: and behind that all those marvellous early lyrical poems and the dazzling appearance he had owned in the thirties, an appearance at once youthful and tragic, that seemed to make him one of the symbols of the age.

'That is irrelevant. I want something from you,' Garner repeated, bravely. 'Something too long or too naughty for anywhere else.'

'You can have some of my Racine translation. It's not naughty but it can be as long as you like.'

'I'd like that,' said Garner. Perhaps it was on people like Clauson he should exercise his powers of editorship. He went on: 'I'd also like you to think of something else – something new for you. Not necessarily verse, or stories.'

'Perhaps,' said Clauson, 'I should do for you what I'm

always threatening myself I shall do – a practical and immediate political and social programme. I shall call it "Towards the Illfare State". I demand low wages for the idle, servants for the deserving, foreign currency for men of good taste, unrationed food for those who prefer reality to the pipe dreams of football pools, the abolition of income tax for the cultured, of pensions for the worn-out, of free medicines for the unhealthy, and of pre-natal clinics for those better unborn.'

'Tut, tut,' said Garner.

'I perceive you are still a vile Whig,' said Clauson. 'But, George, you must agree that any serious magazine ought to give its attention to the stagnation of British life. Stagnation. Every law that is passed is to stop you doing something: every novel, every poem that is published is more timorous, more expected, than the last.'

'The picture's not all black,' mumbled Garner.

'It is *all* black,' said Clauson. 'The only thing that shakes me a little is that someone has found the energy and money to start a magazine. Where *is* the money coming from, by the way?'

'Some eccentric capitalist.'

'There you are!' Clauson held up both his hands as though he were catching a large ball. 'One must create the conditions for eccentricity.'

Clauson's gesture stirred the bottom of Garner's memory – a public meeting years ago at a hall somewhere in Holborn in aid of Republican Spain and Philip Clauson, his head tilted back and the lights burnishing his hair, holding up both his hands at the end of his speech. Garner, too, had been on the platform. It was another world.

'We shall bar politics,' said Garner.

'These aren't politics,' said Clauson. 'These are the simple prerequisites for art.'

'Let's have another gin,' said Garner, ringing the bell. 'And do think seriously of a series for the magazine – a fresh direction or a return to an old one.'

'Just one more and then I must be off.' Clauson fished out a battered cigarette and put it between his beautifully shaped lips that seemed welded on his face and of another, harder material. 'You can have a series of chunks of Racine. I've sworn to write no more prose. Prose says either too little or too much.'

In one of the callboxes in the hall Garner opened the s-z volume of the telephone directory. He could scarcely believe that the number he wanted was really the familiar Whitehall 1212. He ruffled the pages. 'SCOTLAND YARD – SEE POLICE (METROPOLITAN).' He lugged out the L-R volume. It *was* Whitehall 1212. He dialled. The old feeling of apprehension had returned to his stomach.

He said: 'I want to speak to Chief Inspector White.'

'Just a moment, sir.' After a while the voice came back. 'I'm afraid the Chief Inspector isn't here. Will you speak to anyone else?'

'No, thank you,' said Garner. 'I will call again.' He felt enormously and irrationally relieved – as though he had in fact talked to White, as though the whole thing were out of his hands and off his conscience. He came out of the box and lit a cigarette: the gins had made his hands a little numb. The clock said 7.7.

'Call me a taxi, Fred,' he said to the porter. He got his hat from the hooks in the passage off the hall, hearing the thin note of the porter's whistle. Of course, he thought, he need not fear that Sarah would be at Perrott's. He remembered how he had looked desirously at her across the spaces of the Café Royal, and tried to realize that even at that moment her thoughts – her life – must have been embedded in Rackham.

On the steps of the Passengers' he looked quickly but carefully right and left, but Pall Mall seemed to contain only innocent passers-by. He said to the taxi-driver: '9 Temple Gardens. It's somewhere in St John's Wood.'

Chapter Ten

BETWEEN the dim Gothic shapes of two large nineteenth-century houses was a white wall with a rather pretentious tall wrought-iron gate. Beyond the gate was a short paved garden, and beyond the garden a low white modern house of which an estate agent might have used the adjective 'bijou'. Garner was admitted by a foreign manservant with bad teeth, and shown into an L-shaped sitting-room. On its white-painted walls was a series of Rouault etchings: opposite the fireplace a radio-gramophone whose only vulgarism was its enormous bulk. Claude Perrott rose to greet Garner from a settee upholstered in a rough material the colour of aubergines. Garner, horrified, saw that he was wearing a dinner jacket.

'Very good of you to have come at such short notice,' said Perrott.

'Not at all. Delighted.' And Garner added in a growling tone: 'Sorry I haven't dressed. Been busy right up to coming.'

'Don't worry about that, my dear fellow. Sit down here. What will you drink?'

'Oh, gin and something,' said Garner. The manservant hovered anxiously. 'Gin and orange.' Garner crossed his legs and furtively pulled up the thick sock he found bunched round his ankle.

Perrott looked at Garner and revolved the cigar between his lips. 'It's most unfortunate', he said, 'that our friend Fox can't come.'

'Oh, can't he?' said Garner, alarmed. Surely he was not

doomed to spend an evening with this difficult man alone.

'He didn't tell you?' said Perrott. 'Some family occasion, I think, which arose after our arrangements were made and which he couldn't avoid. But he should have let you know.'

'A pity,' said Garner, feelingly and ambiguously, and took a deep swig of his drink.

'Yes,' said Perrott. 'But I look forward to a tête-à-tête with you about our affairs.' Perrott's eyes never left Garner's face: the calm, intent, unembarrassed stare was a trick, as Garner knew, but a trick that worked continually. Garner opened his mouth to blurt out that really he had done nothing towards the magazine, but was forestalled by the entry of a thin, middle-aged woman wearing a saffron-coloured evening gown quite without chic, and carrying a large workbag.

Perrott said: 'I'd like you to meet my wife, Garner. This is Mr Garner, my dear, the novelist.'

'How d'you do, Mr Garner.' Mrs Perrott settled her trailing crêpe into an easy chair. 'You have a great admirer in my son.'

'Ah,' said Garner. 'That is very – er – gratifying.'

'He is an enthusiastic novel reader,' said Mrs Perrott. 'He inherits that from me. But I have never been able to read modern novels. For me, the novel lost its charm when Wells and those people took to it. You know, Mr Garner – purpose and all that sort of thing. I like a novel to have a good plot. I sometimes read Mrs Henry Wood, though they tell me that she is a very bad novelist and quite out of fashion. But she always has an interesting plot – usually about missing wills.'

'Well,' said Garner, 'I'm afraid we don't go in for missing wills these days.'

'I think it's a great pity,' said Mrs Perrott. 'Wills are still important, aren't they? I mean in spite of extortionate death duties and all that sort of thing.'

'At the moment you'll find that the wills have gone to ground in the detective story,' said Garner, manfully keeping his end up.

'Alas,' said Mrs Perrott, 'I've never been able to bring myself to read detective stories. Detectives – so uninteresting a class of men I always imagine. But I'm really talking too much, aren't I, Claude?'

Perrott blew out a thin stream of smoke.

Mrs Perrott went on: 'I'll just do a few stitches of my embroidery before dinner, and let you men get on with your discussions. Now, Mr Garner, you have an aesthetic sense: what will go with this rather difficult solid patch of maroon?'

Garner bent forward conscientiously to give his opinion. As soon as his head got near her he smelt whisky and involuntarily he looked up at her face. He saw that she was rather older than he had imagined: under her powder a veil of discontinuous red veins spread from the wings of her nose to form a dense, glazed flush under her watery eyes. He lowered his glance quickly. The woman was stewed.

'What do you think, Mr Garner?' she asked.

He sensed that she knew he had tumbled to her, that always she was prepared for her new acquaintances, after a few seconds, to readjust their conception; prepared to accept their inadequately concealed disgust, their rudeness even. He said: 'The gold, perhaps?'

'Oh, Mr Garner,' said Mrs Perrott, 'how very bold!'

Garner sat back in his chair, knowing that Perrott's gaze was still on him. He tried to divine the relationship between this pair, and failed – feeling that the character of the man existed in terms beyond his understanding. He remembered at their first meeting the unemotional pat which Perrott had bestowed on Sarah. He thought of the incessant cigars, the tortured Rouaults – as though they might be symbols brought forth by psycho-analysis. He tried to imagine a muscular ambition working in the realms of money and power; and this long marriage which the man had survived in such good – even youthful – shape, and which seemed to have destroyed the woman.

'Have another gin and orange,' said Perrott to Garner, pausing before the last word as though it had been 'arsenic'. When Garner assented Perrott served the drink himself, the manservant having vanished. While he was at the tray of decanters and glasses he said: 'Will you have a drink, my dear?' and the question hung on the air like an insult.

Mrs Perrott did not look up from her embroidery. 'No,' she said. 'No, I don't think I will.'

Garner was embarrassed by the nakedness of the situation: to cover it up he cast round desperately for a topic of conversation. 'Your radiogram looks very interesting,' he said.

'Are you fond of music, Mr Garner?' asked Mrs Perrott.

'Yes,' said Garner, 'especially fond of it in private – away from the discomforts and the irritating people one always finds in concert halls. Really, as mechanical reproduction improves one can almost visualize the end of public performances of music – performances, also, which usually do not attract one because in order to gather an audience they are composed mainly of commonplace items. Who is going out on a November night to sit next to a pimply youth who beats time with his head to the Grieg

Concerto when he can listen before his own fireside to almost as realistic a performance of a quartet by Arriaga?'

Before anyone needed to try to reply to this the manservant returned, showed his bad teeth, and said: 'Dinner iss sairved.' As he got up Garner marvelled at the remote, incomprehensible intellectual snobbery that had caused him to use the name of Arriaga in his little homily. No wonder he could make nothing of Mr and Mrs Perrott.

As the expensive foods succeeded each other it seemed to Garner that the atmosphere in the dining-room grew more and more stifling. Mrs Perrott's volubility subsided: in the end she picked at her food in a light stupor, trying again and again to push permanently back the wisps of greying gingerish hair which kept falling down from the back of her unmodish coiffure. Perrott, seated under the one picture – a splendid early Utrillo landscape – ate and drank with quiet, thorough relish. Garner found his thoughts constantly prowling back to subjects that took his appetite away – Rackham's hand hard on his arm, the figure by his side at the bookshop: or ranging to the disquieting, uncomfortable future – his return to the impermanent room at the Passengers'. When he considered seriously what his action ought to be he felt the sweat of indecision gather in the bends behind his knees, and he burst suddenly into conversation to relieve his anxiety.

That conversation seemed deliberately to avoid the magazine. Perrott talked of a business trip he had just taken to South Africa; he made an elaborate comparison of the situation and amenities of the various airports he had ever had occasion to use; he gave an appreciation of the qualities of a celebrated barrister who had represented his organization in some recent litigation. In all this he showed a clear and, Garner thought, a quite simple mind: his opinions were forceful but unoriginal: he ventured into no realms that were not concrete. It was only the smooth face of faded brown, the pale eyes, that were always turned to one incuriously but watchfully; only the unhurried gestures, the complete absence of self-consciousness or doubt, that betrayed the real man – the man whose total presence impressed and even alarmed.

At last Mrs Perrott's scarcely touched angel-on-horseback was removed. She said: 'I don't think I'll have any dessert.' She rose and the two men rose with her. 'I believe I shall watch the television, my dear,' she said to Perrott. Again the words lingered with significance between husband and wife as though, Garner thought, 'watch the television' were a euphemism for Mrs Perrott's vice. Years ago other phrases had had for this couple in the company of others a private significance, but a significance mocking or erotic.

'Good-bye, Mr Garner – if I don't see you again this evening,' said Mrs Perrott. 'Delightful to have met you.'

Garner felt a rush of pity for her. 'Good-bye, Mrs Perrott. It has been a most delicious dinner. And I shall certainly look into Mrs Henry Wood.' As he resumed his seat and the manservant placed a decanter between him and Perrott, he thought that perhaps his pity was really for himself at being abandoned to the ordeal of Perrott's company alone.

'A glass of port, Garner,' said Perrott, passing the decanter.

'Thank you,' said Garner. He poured and tasted, playing the part of a connoisseur. 'Mm. Excellent.'

'Are you fond of port?' Perrott started to peel a pear. His question, though quite without overtones, seemed to Garner immediately to expose the connoisseurship.

'Yes,' said Garner. 'Yes.' And then it was as though his next words were like a forced move at some complicated game. 'A pity Fox couldn't come. I'd like to have had his thoughts about the magazine.'

'Ah, yes – the magazine.' Perrott spoke as if this were the introduction of some strange and even irrelevant theme in their relationship. His knife halted under a sliver of pear skin as he considered the subject. And then all he said was: 'I'm interested to hear you call it a "magazine". That term for me connotes something quite popular and commercial.'

Garner gave a dutiful little laugh and tried again. 'I'm afraid I haven't got much forrader with it yet.'

'Naturally,' said Perrott. 'After all, it was only Tuesday that we met before.'

But Garner struggled on. 'I've settled with Cuffs about, the production side of things.'

'Splendid.' Perrott cut his pear in half.

'And I've been sounding one or two people about the kind of contributions we want. Philip Clauson, for instance. I don't know what you think of his work.' Garner paused for the comment, but Perrott had his mouth full of pear. 'There's no doubt in my mind,' continued Garner, twirling his port glass rather recklessly, 'that Clauson has still something to say. His poetry has become immensely introspective and arid but it's never lost its sincerity and air of experiment. And I don't really see why he shouldn't produce some prose as important for the times as his poetry books of the thirties were.'

Perrott wiped his lips. 'Very interesting.' He sipped his port. 'I'm quite confident, Garner, that you have the right ideas about our little joint enterprise.'

Garner felt flattered and the desire to flatter in return. 'When I saw Clauson I may say that he was surprised and impressed that this opportunity for a fresh literary advance had been conceived and made possible by a – an industrialist.'

Perrott had finished his port and brought out a pig-skin cigar-case. 'Cigar, Garner? Or another glass of port?' Garner chose the cigar. Perrott said: 'I'm not an industrialist, you know, Garner.'

Garner looked rather foolish, and said: 'Oh?'

'My organization is called the Power Industries Protection Corporation,' said Perrott. 'A little way removed from industry itself, as you may guess from its title.'

It seemed to Garner that if he were given a moment to think about it he would find this information significant. But Perrott had risen and was saying: 'Shall we have our coffee in my study and then we can get our business affairs over?' Garner thought that if Perrott was expecting more news of *Light* he was in for a disappointment.

There were two desks in the study, as though for Father Bear and Baby Bear. They were both of bleached maple and both supported angle lamps that looked like Calder mobiles. At the smaller desk, typing on a machine that gave out only the faintest of thuds, sat a girl whose tiny waist, clasped by a narrow gilt belt, could be seen through the aperture of her grey-sprayed metal chair.

Perrott said: 'I think you've met our little Miss Freeman, Garner.'

Garner nodded and Sarah turned and smiled politely at him as though nothing had happened since that day she had ushered him out of the anteroom at Power House. The manservant had followed them in with a tray. Perrott said: 'Would you like some coffee, Miss Freeman?' Sarah said she would. The manservant poured and Perrott let fall a few remarks: it was the trivial domestic preliminary to some drama on an intenser plane. Garner saw the manservant depart with the panic felt by the deathbed visitor at the exit of the nurse.

'And I'm not really sure that I enjoy looking at it across foolscap sheets, between an ashtray and an inkwell,' Perrott was saying. He leaned across his desk and stroked the rough bronze Degas figurine of a girl bending over, her hands clasping the knees of her straight legs.

'No, I quite see that,' said Gardner, abstractedly. He suddenly felt asinine holding the thick cigar and the frail coffee cup. It seemed to him that he had really known of, that with rather more careful thought he could have easily formulated (as, after the race is run, one sees the name of the winning horse), Sarah's appearance here – that this visit to Perrott was not a relief from, but a continuation of, the events that had been frightening him. Incongruously he noticed that under the desk Sarah had slipped off one of her shoes: with prurient emotion he saw the dark seam of her stocking running from the folds of her dress to her slim heel, and the pinkness of her sole showing vaguely through the shadowy nylon.

'Well, now,' said Perrott, 'have you drawn Mr Garner's cheque, Miss Freeman?' Sarah shuffled her shoe on and took an enormous cheque-book over for Perrott to sign. Garner looked on with the embarrassment of one who sees that he is about to receive unexpected and undeserved charity. Perrott said, as he scribbled with a fat gold fountain-pen: 'I would like to pay your editor's salary in advance each quarter, Garner – direct to you. Printing and contributors and so on I shall settle through Cuffs, of course.'

'That will be fine,' said Garner. Sarah tore out the cheque and brought it to him. The odour of her perfume was like an event that breaks a dream. That he examined the cheque at all was a tribute to Perrott as a business man. To Garner's bewilderment he saw that it was for £250. He looked at Perrott. 'You said "each quarter" surely.'

Perrott was smiling, and the act gave him a face that Garner had not seen before – the face a boy sees on his headmaster in the presence of his parents. 'For this quarter,' said Perrott, 'I hope you will accept the additional sum. You are going to have a lot of preliminary work and I think it only proper that you should not be out of pocket over it. I'm very glad we have been able to have this meeting tonight: it has given me an excellent idea of the difficulties of your task – and confirmed the resolution I formed some time ago that you should be adequately compensated for the ardours of this first period.'

'Very generous,' Garner managed to get out. But he could not remember speaking a word to Perrott about his difficulties over *Light*.

'Not at all,' said Perrott. 'I'm only too pleased if I've made you feel a little happier, a little easier, about our enterprise. In my crude way I try to value the work of the artist. And, after all, it is the leisure bought by money that enables the artist to create.'

Garner folded the cheque and put it in his pocket.

'Thank you very much,' he said. Sarah came over again, this time with the coffee jug. Perrott put a fresh cigar in his mouth: its colour harmonized with the colour of his face. He said: 'I hope you won't find that the – er – magazine will interfere too much with your own writing, Garner.'

'No,' said Garner. 'I don't think it will interfere at all. I shall give up some of my reviewing. I ought not to review, anyway. Reviewers become either liars or boors, and their work is valueless as well as being impermanent. Reviewing is a drug habit.'

Perrott smiled again. Sarah had gone back to her desk and was separating a sheaf of tops and carbons. Garner looked down at the floor, saw his dusty shoes, and thrust them out of sight under his lime-green leather-and-chromium chair. Perrott glanced at his watch, coughed, and said: 'It's very unfortunate, Garner, but I have to go out. Unpardonably discourteous to you, and I apologize most sincerely. It's an affair which only boiled up yesterday – a poor devil whose company is in the doldrums – and I thought I wouldn't disturb our dinner engagement.'

'That's quite all right,' said Garner. He rose to his feet with an enormous sense of relief. He was not in the least put out that Perrott had had enough of his society and was off to his delayed Saturday-night pleasures. For a fleeting moment he wondered what they were: boys, bridge?

'My dear chap,' said Perrott, 'sit down, sit down. You mustn't think of going yourself. Miss Freeman will entertain you. Perhaps you would like to investigate the radio-gramophone. And I know my wife would be delighted if a little later you honoured her evening tea-tray with your presence.'

Garner sat down. 'That would be splendid,' he said weakly.

Perrott said: 'There's just one thing I must speak to you about before I go, Garner. Miss Freeman tells me that her fiancé is in some sort of trouble, and that, oddly enough, you can help him, Garner.'

The old, painful tension returned to Garner's belly.

'It seems that this young man secured employment in Lancashire. His employer – er – took a fancy to him. You know what I mean, Garner. The young man found the situation intolerable and returned to London. The employer followed. You knew this man, Garner: it must be painful for you. He was very unbalanced. It appears almost certain that he committed suicide. Now – foolishly, in my opinion, but very naturally – Miss Freeman's fiancé kept what he knew to himself. The authorities had no means of connecting him with your friend's unfortunate death. Of course he hoped that the affair would blow over, hoped to keep his name out of what would have been – with all respect – a rather sordid story and one open to great misinterpretation. I think you realize, Garner, that you yourself have become the connecting link.'

'Yes,' said Garner, 'I realize that.' Perrott's calm features, his fluent, persuasive words – the tone of a chairman presenting a bad balance-sheet – almost made him accept the thing as it had been put. Like a baffled debater, he climbed laboriously back over the smooth surface of the argument to look for flaws.

'What good can come, Garner, of revealing this young man's innocent part in this business?' asked Perrott. Garner opened his mouth to speak, but Perrott's voice flowed on. 'Nothing can bring your unhappy friend back to life.

If his – um – weakness became public knowledge great distress would, I'm sure, be caused to his friends and relatives.' Perrott's hands rested monolithically on the desk, one holding the cigar upright, like a torch. 'All that would be achieved would be that a coroner's jury would bring in a verdict of suicide instead of accidental death. I shall esteem it a personal favour, Garner, if you will keep your special knowledge to yourself.' The cigar was taken slowly towards his mouth. Before it quite got there Perrott added: 'I take it, of course, that you haven't divulged it yet.'

Garner felt that his face was very red. 'Wait a minute, wait a minute.' His voice came out hoarse, laden with the local accent of his youth. He was acutely conscious of Sarah's presence, still sitting with her back to them at the little desk. 'I'm very much afraid you haven't got the right story, Perrott.' Garner's mind worked furiously: what *was* the right story? 'This young man – the reason he couldn't be connected with the death was that he'd got the job up north under a false name. Or lives down here under one.'

Once again Perrott smiled. 'Well, now, I've been given a perfectly sensible explanation of that. The reason –'

'No, no!' Garner's tones were loud and rude. 'That's only a minor point. I see now – you haven't mentioned Kershaw. Kershaw knew – knew something – so they disposed of him as well.'

'Kershaw?' Perrott looked towards Sarah with a puzzled air. 'I haven't been briefed about Kershaw. However, let's keep to essentials, Garner.'

Garner was leaning forward and breathing heavily, like a boxer at the start of a new round. But his antagonist was not prepared to fight.

'However you look at it,' Perrott continued, 'nothing good can come of your taking the matter further.'

'I don't know about good, I don't know about good,' said Garner, incoherently.

Perrott said: 'Let's be calm about it. All I am asking you to do is to consider your position very carefully. We have a happy association, you and I, and I hope it will continue. I wanted you and no one else to edit *Light*. I take a warm interest in your career, Garner. Remember that.'

Garner almost instinctively pulled his wallet from his pocket: he took out the cheque and threw it on Perrott's desk. 'I can't take that. I didn't know what it was for,' he said. 'And I can't go on with the magazine.'

'Come, Garner,' Perrott said. 'Look at this thing rationally. You are upset about your friend. But when you have reflected a little I think you will appreciate the difficulties of Miss Freeman's fiancé. You can't bring back the dead, but you can help the living. And put the cheque away, my dear fellow. This business need make no difference between us about our financial arrangements.'

Garner said, in a trembling voice: 'What has Miss Freeman to say?'

'I am speaking for Miss Freeman,' said Perrott.

'Then I think you'd have done better to get the facts from her first.'

Perrott stood up. 'I'm sorry you've felt obliged to adopt this attitude, Garner. I hope you will think about the matter more calmly before you take any further steps. I regret very much that I have to leave you at this juncture.' He came round the desk and held out his hand. 'Good night, Garner.'

Garner rose, looked at the hand, and found no reason

why he should not shake it. It was soft and warm, the grip firm. Garner muttered a good night.

At the door Perrott turned and said: 'It might help if you had a little discussion with Miss Freeman.'

The bars of the electric fire inset in the wall glowed through the cigar smoke. The room was very hot. Into the silence came the sound of the shutting of the front door and the starting of a car engine. Garner thought: What a fool I was not to have remembered to tell him about Trimmer. Sarah swung round from the desk and looked at him out of a blank face.

'I didn't tell him about Trimmer,' he said to her angrily.

'What was the point?'

He blundered towards the door. 'Where will my hat be?'

She said: 'So you didn't go to the police this afternoon.'

'I refuse to talk to you about it,' he said with foolish dignity.

'Were you too frightened, or not frightened enough?'

'Go to hell.'

She went over to him. 'George, I honestly think if you forget about it all nothing will happen.'

Her seriousness alarmed him afresh. 'What do you mean?' he said uneasily.

'Did you believe him, then?'

'Believe Rackham? I never spoke to him.'

'Perrott, Perrott!' she cried. 'Don't you understand anything?'

He wiped his forehead with the palm of his hand. One goes in the cinema in the middle of a film: when it comes round again, knowing the neat end-pattern of plot, one sees the improbable strands gradually weaving themselves into positions less improbable. 'Yes,' he said. 'Yes, I think I do.'

'You must do,' she said. Her eyes were fastened on him as though he had drawn the lot for a terrible mission.

'It was Perrott who wanted me as editor,' he said. 'Not Fox.' And then he added quickly: 'Perrott put Fox off from coming here tonight.'

She said: 'Can't you get it into your head that the police could never protect you?'

He saw, as a conscript sees the ponderous but delicate military machine that reaches out and draws his individuality into its complicated anonymity, the force that had made sure that it owned Widgery's 'best friend', confidant, executor.

He found he was still holding the dead butt of his cigar. He put it carefully in the great ashtray on Perrott's desk, and then looked round at the door as though he were fearful that Perrott might have silently returned and been standing there. The vision came to him of the little room at Askington, the rather pathetic rack of test-tubes and the length of old carpet on the floor.

'What had Widgery discovered?' The point came out easily and almost casually, as though it were some trivial question he might, had he remembered, have asked her long before.

'I think it was a virtually indestructible filament. For lamps and valves.' She stood with her thighs pressed against the desk, her face averted now.

'And he wouldn't play with – with the big people.'

'I don't know. I suppose not. Peter had to go up there.'

'My God,' said Garner. And then he forgot Widgery and said: 'And you inveigled me to that party for Rackham to make sure Kershaw hadn't blabbed and that I hadn't seen him killed. You betrayed me.' He thought: All the time Perrott has been playing with this idea of a magazine which I have been taking so desperately seriously. He ground his teeth with anger, and said: 'And Perrott', and could get nothing else out.

She said: 'I don't know what he meant me to tell you. I know he means to prevent you from telling what you've discovered. He can't care whether you know about him ...'

'How can I not tell?' Garner almost wrung his hands. 'Two men have been murdered.'

Suddenly she turned to him and pressed her head into his green knitted waistcoat. He put his arms round her and held her gently. Under the frock she felt as unexpectedly warm as a bird. She said something unintelligible in a choked voice which he didn't bother to elucidate. He was thinking that this was what Perrott had gone out and left them for. He said: 'So that's what you arrange in your nice offices on the Embankment.'

She stepped away from him and said: 'There have been other things, but not this.'

'Who drove the lorry?'

'I don't know. It may have been an accident. So may the other. I honestly don't know, George.'

'I know,' said Garner. 'I bloody know.'

'Don't go to the police.'

'It may have been an accident, but you think Rackham will hang.'

'Why should I have told you all I have if it was only Peter I was thinking about?'

Garner laughed theatrically. 'You don't want me to believe that you're trying to protect *me*?'

As she turned her head a light flashed momentarily through the lens of moisture in her eye. 'I want it all to end. More than anything I want it to end.'

He looked at her, her features that had the power to present themselves, like some large and classic painting, with continually fresh and moving elements to his conception, and wished remotely that their history could be altered. He said: 'What a crew!' and abruptly opened the door into the passage.

The passage led into the hall at the far end of which Garner saw Mrs Perrott emerge from the sitting-room, self-absorbed, trance-like, her hair further disarranged. She walked across the hall without seeing them, and disappeared up the stairs. Sarah opened the door of a closet and Garner saw his hat on a hook next to a bowler. Life had resumed its normality: it was as though the study had been a stage on which they had all been playing melodramatic parts. Now he felt utterly tired – so tired that when he looked at Sarah's face again he saw its paleness, clarity, with a complete absence of emotion. It was the face of a stranger he was not going to summon up the energy to get to know. She said good-bye: he did not reply.

Chapter Eleven

IN Temple Gardens the wind swayed the bough of a tree across a street lamp so that its light came like that of a guttering candle. The road was deserted. Garner was not sure where precisely he was: he had not followed the route his taxi had taken. At a venture he turned right and walked along hurriedly, hugging the wall. 'I want a taxi,' he said to himself, and visualized hailing one, saying 'The Passengers' Club', and climbing into the safe little womb.

In the echo of his footfalls he thought he could hear the sound of other footfalls, but when he stopped there was complete silence. But perhaps the other had stopped simultaneously. He walked on and then halted again, this time abruptly. Again there was silence.

In the darkness between two streetlamps he encountered a standing figure and his heart gave a sickening dive. But almost at once he saw that the man was holding a dog on a lead, waiting for it to fulfil some natural need. Garner passed, whistling through his teeth. He found he could not connect the sounds into a tune.

This end of the street debouched into a little square. He could not see, through the trees in the centre, whether or not there was a way through it. He was frightened that it might be a cul-de-sac and that he would have to go back the whole length of Temple Gardens. After a moment's indecision he turned into a passage which ran to the right, just before the start of the houses in the square. Halfway down, a lamp bracketed to the wall showed the entrance to a mews that obviously ran along the rear of Temple Gardens. The passage itself ended in a semicircle of garage doors. It was fate that had made him choose the passage: as he wheeled hurriedly, apprehensively, to retrace his steps he saw his pursuer silhouetted against the comparative brightness of Temple Gardens, and recognized in himself the strange element of voluntariness in the terrified victim. For a moment Garner stopped and looked at the running man, as for a moment one tastes without movement or sound the onset of a frightful pain. And then he dashed wildly down the mews.

As he caught his foot in some irregularity, staggered, half recovered with a clawing motion at the air, and finally sprawled violently across the cobbles, it seemed to him that this action, too, was fated – that with a little more control he could have prevented it, just as once, long ago, when his father had ferociously beaten him, he had, quite of his own volition and yet compulsively, allowed his cries and tears to emerge. He tried now, with gasps that seemed to him exaggerated, too painful, to get his breath back. He saw his hat lying on the ground a few feet ahead of him. He decided to leave it behind.

Then he heard Trimmer come up. He thought: They won't kill me here. But he didn't believe that they would kill him at all. He could not imagine that they would even hurt him. So that when Trimmer hit him across the ear he cried, not in a loud voice: 'Oh no.'

He found he could get to his feet. Trimmer was standing in front of him: even in the gloom it could be seen that he wore the brim of his hat turned all the way down, and that he carried a stick. He was holding the stick handily halfway down its length. Suddenly Garner felt a great hatred of Trimmer. He lunged forward towards him, with fists and teeth clenched. Trimmer hit him in the mouth.

Garner fell on his hands and knees, and then his arms gave way. He felt Trimmer kick him in the pit of the stomach and wanted above anything else to say that the blow in the face was enough, that these other blows that went on and on were not necessary. Instead of hatred he began to feel a great love for Trimmer that he would have liked to tell him about, a love that he could have shown absurdly but sincerely by kissing Trimmer's shoes. His breathing seemed to have become very loud, and then he realized that he was groaning.

When he managed at last to get to his feet, Trimmer had gone. There was a dog barking somewhere in the direction of the square. It had been like a rape: the protagonists in strenuous unspeaking intimacy. Garner found that he was constantly spitting out. There were some hard sharp fragments between his gums and lips and on his tongue. When he realized that they were fragments of teeth his legs trembled so violently that he had to support himself on a dustbin that stood against the wall. And then to his surprise he was sick. Bending wretchedly forward he thought: This is myself.

Afterwards he still had to go on spitting. It appeared that the action satisfied a psychological as well as a physical need. He was tough, he was spitting out teeth as nonchalantly as the hero of a half-remembered story read in childhood. He rose slowly from the dustbin and went to look for his hat. He said to himself, as though he were consoling himself, that it must have been a knuckleduster. His hat touched the ear Trimmer had hit, the ear that seemed as large as the cardboard kind sold at the joke shop in New Oxford Street: gently he explored the sogginess inside. When he looked at his finger it wore a dark thimble of blood.

Finally, he dared to bring his tongue forward from where it had lain curled in terror, and pass it quickly the first time and then again slowly, with a growing horror, over the jagged gap at the front of his mouth.

In the alley he had brushed down his clothes, hidden his disarranged hair under his hat, and made his handkerchief into a pad to hold in front of his lips. He had thought that he could not go to the Passengers' in the state he was in, and then had understood that there was no need to. So he had walked painfully until he found himself in Regent's Park Road, and at last had hailed his taxi.

And now it was taking him round the familiar square to his flat – all the more familiar because it seemed an epoch since he had walked out of it to make his telephone call at Marble Arch. From his stomach and ribs flowed a sick ache: the palms of his hands burned where he had taken the skin off as he fell: a pulse beat heavily in his head. The blood in his ear made him partially deaf.

The taxi stopped: he put up his handkerchief, got out, and paid the driver. The man said: 'Ta', and then: 'Feeling all right, mate?' Garner nodded, turned, and rushed up the steps towards the loneliness he desired and yet feared. At the door of his flat he felt for his key – without success, and he realized that during those minutes in the mews it had fallen out of his pocket or he had unknowingly pulled it out with his handkerchief. It was a fresh violation: he stood helplessly on the landing, tears springing to his eyes. There was nothing for it but to go down to the basement flat. He arranged his handkerchief in a larger mask, pulled his hat over his eyes, and descended the stairs. He tried to dull his excruciating sensitivity about his appearance by concentrating on the stair rail, his slow progress, the dust-loaded pattern of the wallpaper.

It was Marjorie who opened the door. When he remembered that she could not see him he lowered the handkerchief with a sense of enormous relief. He said: 'Garner here. Afraid I've lost my key. Could I borrow the one you have?' To his alarm he found himself almost unable to pronounce some of the words: in his effort to get them out he found his mouth and tongue making the convulsive motions he had sometimes observed in the aged.

'Hello, Mr Garner,' the girl said. 'Just a sec – it's in my overall pocket.'

He leaned against the door jamb while she went confidently down the passage. When she came back and he had to straighten up to reach for the key, he felt the nausea rise from his stomach and the world took on the scratchily grey surface of an early film. He clutched at her to stop himself falling. 'Hey up,' she said.

In a moment or two the colours and sounds came back. He released her shoulders and said: 'I'm sorry. I'm not feeling well.'

'I should think not,' she said.

Seeing her eyes directed blankly towards his chest, he gained a little confidence. 'I've had an accident,' he announced.

'Oh,' she said, her sympathy suddenly enveloping him. 'I'm sorry.'

'I fell,' he said. 'It was very stupid. But I'm rather shaken up.'

'Why don't you come in for a minute and have a cup of tea? They're both at the pictures and the kids are in bed.'

'No,' he said, shying off again. 'No, I don't think I will. Thank you all the same.'

'As a matter of fact there's a cup made. It'll save you bothering.'

It came to him as a luxurious idea that his condition demanded the balm of tea. 'All right,' he said. 'It's very kind of you.'

As they went together towards the kitchen she said: 'Do you know, at first I thought you were tight. Your speech – and everything.'

The tea hurt his mouth, but he went on sipping, as though he were anxious to prove the efficacy of her attention towards him. She had put him in the only chair that bore a semblance of comfort, near a small cheap electric fire that stood away from the empty hearth on the shiny flowered linoleum. The square table was covered with worn oilcloth: on it, next to her own cup and saucer, was an open volume in Braille. She had pulled a chair from the table and sat on it, facing him. He said through the steam: 'This is comforting.'

'I'm glad,' she said. She always held her pale face very still and tilted upwards, the straight brown hair falling back a little, as if to make up for her blindness she were listening intently. She brought her cigarette high to her mouth and took a drag of it. She said, making it a statement: 'You hurt yourself very much.'

He put his cup back on the saucer which stood on the mantelpiece at his shoulder. For a moment he thought wildly of rushing over to her and burying his face in her lap. And then quite deliberately he controlled himself and took up his cup again. 'Yes,' he said. He wondered whether he should add what was in his mind, but before he could decide rationally it came out. 'You're always very acute about people.' She blushed. He thought how strange it was to be looking at her so calculatingly, as though he were hidden and she going unconsciously about her affairs. Under her white blouse of thin, trashy stuff he could see two sets of shoulder straps indicating two undergarments, and he asked himself, imagining the steps she might take, whether he could ever find her desirable. And then once again he ran his tongue along his shattered teeth and the panic returned and rose to a crescendo in his chest. He must go, he must go.

'Well,' he said, with casual and false calm. 'I must go and let you get on with your reading.' She rose, emanating that sense of slight thwarted expectation that he so often thought he discerned in his acquaintances. What did she want from him? She had flinched from that physical contact at the door, she always denied his efforts at sympathy. But now it was his own demands which had to be investigated: he saw her retreat beyond the circle of his feeling to the cold region of politeness and convention. 'Thank you so much,' he said.

As soon as he had switched on the light and closed the door his eyes flew across the room to the mirror. Then he slowly hung up his hat, as though there were someone watching him to whom he had to prove his indifference to the reflection that awaited him. He walked over to the fireplace.

The face was not his, and yet he must own it. His heart thudded as his fingers explored, probed. He had not in his worst moments expected that he would be quite changed. He told himself that the bruising and the swelling would go; that tomorrow – no, Monday – he would be able to telephone the dentist; that after a little while the façade of himself would be erected again. He tried to think – as when he had accidentally broken some valued possession – that it did not really matter, that enormously skilful repairs were perfectly possible, that in any event what he had previously valued so much was not, after all, valuable. For a moment he conceived that he might, even at 10.30 on a Saturday night, speak to his dentist, confess to the shattered mouth, discover just what he had permanently to bear.

Some vomit, he saw, had dried in his beard. He went sadly to the sink, took off his jacket and tie, and bathed his face in warm water. He put on his dressing-gown, but the familiar gesture brought no comfort. He picked up his jacket and took from his wallet the letter he had written to Viola Widgery in the Passengers'. The sight of the wallet reminded him that he had left his cheque for £250 in Perrott's study. He saw the magazine now like the Corporations of Fascism, a theoretical conception which had scarcely more than hovered on the brink of existence, and he marvelled at his past belief in it.

Garner sat down at his desk and opened the letter. He was appalled at its total misconception of the situation. He tore it up into small fragments, unscrewed his pen, and pulled a sheet of paper towards him. He wrote his address, the date, and then 'My dear' – there was hardly a pause – 'Miss Widgery: The London Library people were very helpful. They told me that *"Maud" Vindicated* had been borrowed by Alan Laybourne. By an odd chance I happen to know Laybourne slightly – he's a man of about my age, a lecturer in English at London University, quite a good critic. So I went to see him. It seems that his parents live near Askington and he spent part of the Easter vacation with them. He took *"Maud" Vindicated* with him – he's doing a piece on Tennyson for the Third Programme – had missed it since he got back, but had been hoping it would turn up. He admitted that he often loses books – and other things! – and when I told him my story he thought that he might very well have left poor Maud in a pub or café in Askington. My guess is that William picked it up with the intention of sending it to the London Library – he may even have found it in the street.

'I'm afraid that disposed of our last chance of finding Rogers. The more I think about the whole affair, the more I feel that it all lies in the realm of accident and coincidence. I trust that in time you will be able to delete from your memory – '

Garner laid down his pen in order to light a cigarette. He hoped that he had cast off for ever the intolerable burden of responsibility and duty that his relationship with Viola had demanded that he should bear.

He thought, as he smoked, how precisely Perrott (or Rackham) had gauged the thing – just that amount of violence at just that particular time, and Garner had been disposed of, written off, forgotten. It was probable, perhaps, that he was still under surveillance, but even that would soon end, and they would rest easily in their knowledge of his complete cowardice. The alien machine into which he had accidentally dropped from his own harmless world had thrown him out again, broken, with scarcely any damage or interruption to its purposive wheels.

Under its smarts and throbbing his body was utterly

exhausted. Only his mind ran on, darting from scene to scene, humiliation to humiliation, and returning always to the obsession of his disfigurement. He made an audible sound of pain.

A little later he heard a faint scratching at the door. For a moment the noise petrified him with fear. Then he got up and opened the door a few inches. The downstairs cat squeezed slowly through the aperture and took a few nonchalant steps into the room. Garner shut the door and went down on his hands and knees. 'Hello,' he said, in a voice loaded with tenderness. 'What do *you* want?' The cat purred and paced a short way backwards and forwards. Garner stroked its small black wedge of head. He felt its cool nose on the rawness of his palm, and then its tongue came out and licked with relish the colourless ichor from his wound.

He got up and went towards the kitchen for some milk, calling the cat as he went. He recalled a scene after the death of his mother: his father sitting weeping in a chair, pulling him – a child of eight – against his wet cheek and moustache, and saying brokenly: 'You're all I've got now, Georgie.' Garner poured some milk in a saucer and put it on the floor. As the cat came up to lap it, he bent down and whispered softly, in his new lisping, ridiculous voice, in the creature's ear.